CAROLINE CORBY was born and brought up in London. She studied mathematics and statistics at Bristol University, then became a banker and spent thirteen years in the City, ending up as a director in a venture capital company before deciding to leave her job to spend more time with her young family.

Caroline has always enjoyed history and wanted to find a historical novel aimed at children that would capture her daughters' imagination. After searching without success, she decided to write one herself and the Before They Were Famous series was born. It explores the early lives of some of history's most fascinating characters who, in shifting dangerous worlds, struggle to make their mark and become heroes and heroines of the future. Of *Lady Jane Grey: Queen for Sale*, Caroline says: "The more I researched Jane's life, the sadder I found it. It's hard to imagine how her parents could have been so cruel."

Caroline lives in Hampstead, North London, with her husband and three daughters, aged sixteen, fourteen and twelve.

Other titles in the series

CAROLINE CORBY

Lady Jane Grey

Queen for Sale

WALKER
BOOKS

First published in Great Britain 2010 by Walker Books Ltd
87 Vauxhall Walk, London SE11 5HJ

2 4 6 8 10 9 7 5 3 1

Text © 2010 Caroline Corby
Cover design © 2010 Walker Books Ltd

The right of Caroline Corby to be identified as author of this
work has been asserted by her in accordance with the
Copyright, Designs and Patents Act 1988

This book has been typeset in Quercus and Ludovico Woodcut

Printed in Great Britain by Clays Ltd, St Ives plc

British Library Cataloguing in Publication Data:
a catalogue record for this book is
available from the British Library

ISBN 978-1-4063-1255-3

www.walker.co.uk

For my grandmother, Pat

January 1547,
in the reign of
King Henry VIII

Bradgate Hall, Leicestershire

"Henry, where are you?" Jane heard her mother shout, and then a door slammed, shaking the window panes in the grand bedroom. She glanced around despairingly. Precious skirts, jackets and petticoats were scattered over a large bed. She grabbed the nearest dress, a sumptuous crimson gown, and tried to stuff it back into an oak chest, but it was too bulky and soon became crumpled. Jane's heart began to pound. Lady Dorset had said she would be out until supper but here she was, bellowing at the top of her voice, and the clock hadn't yet struck midday.

In a panic Jane ran this way and that, gathering things up. She'd been told to hem a dress but the temptation to pull out her mother's gowns and stroke the soft rich material had proved too strong and now there were clothes everywhere. How could she have been so foolish?

"Mistress Ellen, have you seen my husband?"

Her mother sounded alarmingly close. Jane stopped what she was doing and clasped her hands together fervently praying, *Dear God, please don't let her come in here.*

"He left a few hours ago, madam." Mistress Ellen

sounded flustered. No doubt she'd also thought Lady Dorset was gone for the day. "Perhaps he went to visit Sir Howarth."

"Then send a groom to Groby Hall. Tell him to come home at once. I have news."

The doorhandle turned. *Oh no!* thought Jane. She looked frantically around the chamber for somewhere to hide, then pulled her skirt close and slipped behind the thick damask curtains just as the heavy door creaked open.

"What on earth...!" shrieked her mother.

"What is it, madam?" asked Mistress Ellen, hurrying in.

"I told her to mend my dress, not scatter clothes everywhere. If she's damaged anything..."

Jane heard heavy footsteps and then the curtain was wrenched back.

"Come here!" her mother thundered, grabbing her arm. "Explain this mess!"

Lady Dorset had a hefty bosom, a thick neck and a broad face. She was lavishly dressed in a doublet and long skirt of russet velvet with a matching hat.

"I only wanted to look at your beautiful things..." stammered Jane.

A stinging slap on her cheek sent her tumbling to the ground. She lay still for a moment tasting blood in her mouth and then her mother kicked her hard in the stomach.

"Madam, please stop," twittered Mistress Ellen as she

ran about the room, frantically folding clothes. "This mess will soon be cleared up."

But Lady Dorset was in too much of a frenzy to listen. Her eyes were wild and cruel as she rained down blows on her daughter.

"Stop, madam! You'll exhaust yourself," begged Mistress Ellen and at last it did seem Lady Dorset was worn out for she slumped to the ground, her skirt puffing up around her.

Although her stomach hurt and she was dazed and shaky, Jane knew she mustn't move. She must do nothing to provoke another thrashing.

"Come and lie down, madam," said the nurse, helping Lady Dorset to her feet and guiding her to the enormous four-poster bed.

Mistress Ellen was a hunched-up elderly woman with a downy chin and currant eyes. A white linen cloth covered her hair and she wore a plain wool dress and pinafore. Compared to her mistress she was tiny, but she sat Lady Dorset down and pulled off her muddy riding boots, cooing soothingly, "I'll get one of the maids to bring you a cup of beer, madam. You need rest."

"Mistress Ellen, you're right," sighed Lady Dorset. "I am a little strained. But I must see Henry."

"Of course, madam," said the nurse, pulling back the counterpane. "I'll send Ferdinand to fetch him straight away. His Lordship will be back within the hour. Now try to sleep."

Lady Dorset allowed herself to be tucked into bed. As Mistress Ellen drew the curtains she signalled to Jane. Slowly, trembling, Jane got to her feet and crept towards the door. As she eased the latch, Lady Dorset rolled over and moaned, "Mistress Ellen, my daughter provokes me. It's her fault I lose my temper."

"I know, madam," replied the nurse. "I'll see she keeps out of your way."

Jane slipped from the room. *If only that were possible,* she thought forlornly. She would like nothing better than to leave Bradgate Hall and never see either of her parents again. But she was too valuable; they would never let her go.

Sore and still shocked, Jane made her way down the grand staircase. At the bottom was a large hall with an ornate wooden ceiling, oak pannelling on the walls and a dresser covered with silver cups, tankards and plates.

As she reached the last step, Jane caught sight of herself in the polished steel mirror over the fireplace. Her auburn hair was tangled, her freckled face pale and her left cheek was beginning to swell. It was so humiliating. All the servants who scurried around Bradgate Hall knew Lady Dorset beat her horribly. As they dressed Jane, the maids never commented on the purple and blue blotches that disfigured her limbs, but their lingering eyes didn't miss a thing and they told the scullery boys, who told the grooms and the gardeners. Jane knew this from their pitying looks. Her mother might be the king's favourite niece, and Jane might sleep in a fancy bedchamber, wear fine clothes and eat rich food, but none of the servants envied her. None would willingly have taken her place.

Gingerly she touched her face. The slightest pressure made it throb. She would be bruised for days. *I wish Ferdinand was here*, she thought. He was her only friend, the one person she could confide in, but he would already be on his way to Groby Hall with strict instructions to bring her father home as soon as possible.

She heard footsteps in the corridor and, unable to face an embarrassed stare at her scarlet cheek, crept quickly into the cloakroom. There the row of heavy woollen capes gave her an idea. Rather than wait for Ferdinand to return, she would go and meet him.

She pulled her black cloak from its peg, tucked her hair under the hood, swapped her velvet slippers for sturdier walking boots and slipped outside into the courtyard.

On the far side of the rose-red brick mansion, just beyond the west wing of the house, was a gate tucked into a hedge. It led to the formal gardens, although the ornamental box hedges were now hidden by drifting snow. The fountains and ponds were frozen, but the sky was a beautiful crisp blue and there wasn't a breath of wind.

Jane snapped off a finger-sized icicle from a sundial, pressed it to her tender cheek and then made her way around the lumpy, snow-covered flowerbeds and the kitchen garden with its thin winter pickings of carrots, turnips and cabbages, before heading off into the huge park.

Being away from her wretched home made her feel calmer. With each step, her legs grew steadier and her aches and pains dulled until she could almost put the thrashing and the vicious, wild look in her mother's eyes out of her mind.

She trudged on. The rolling moors twinkled prettily in the sunlight but the snow made walking heavy going. The hem of her velvet dress was soon soaked and her feet were cold, but she plodded on towards a distant oak, close to the path Ferdinand would take.

At last she reached the tree, cleared snow from a nearby rock, pulled her cape close and settled down to wait. It wasn't long before a horse with a stocky rider cantered through the next field. Her father, Lord Dorset, was racing home. Jane didn't move and a while later a boy in breeches, riding boots and a sheepskin doublet came riding towards her. After delivering his message, Ferdinand must have stopped to visit his mother who worked in the kitchens of Groby Hall.

Jane stood up waving both arms and was relieved when Ferdinand slowed his horse and trotted over, the bright snow highlighting the olive skin, black hair and dark eyes he'd inherited from his Spanish mother.

"What are you doing here, Jane? You must be frozen," he said, and then he noticed her cheek. "What happened? Was it your mother again?"

Jane hated talking about her beatings, even with Ferdinand.

"It was partly my fault. I thought she was going to be out and—"

"You shouldn't make excuses for her."

"All mothers hit their children."

"Not like her," interrupted Ferdinand. "That woman's a

witch – and now she'll have even more to scheme about."

"What do you mean?"

Ferdinand looked surprised.

"Haven't you heard? The king died three days ago."

"The king is dead!"

Jane slumped back down on the rock. This must be the news her mother was so excited about. But it was almost impossible to believe – King Henry had ruled England and Wales for nearly forty years.

Several years ago he'd visited Bradgate Hall. Jane still remembered a vast lumbering man with thighs like tree trunks, a wide flabby face and sharp grey eyes. He was dressed in yards and yards of the richest brocades, silks and furs, and accompanied by a huge retinue of courtiers, servants and soldiers. But what made the strongest impression on her was that throughout his five-day visit everyone in the household was terrified.

Normally if she crept into the kitchen, the cooks would give her a handful of currants or a slice of fruitcake, but during King Henry's visit she was crossly shooed away. Even her mother, always so imperious and haughty, had jumped at his every command.

One evening Jane asked Mistress Ellen why everyone was so scared of the king and she had never forgotten her reply. "Your great uncle is the most powerful man in the country. If anyone displeases him, no matter how rich, he has them killed. He's even beheaded two of his own wives. So mind you behave or I won't be held accountable for the consequences."

"So now it's Edward's turn," she said at last.

"Do you know Prince— I mean King Edward?" asked Ferdinand, quickly rectifying his error.

Jane smiled. Ferdinand was always so correct. That was the first thing she'd noticed about him when he'd joined the household a year ago and began accompanying her on her daily ride in the park. He'd always called her "miss", never met her eye and stayed exactly five paces behind, tugging frantically at his reins if she slowed unexpectedly. This went on for months, until one morning in spring when she was cantering across a hay field and her pony reared up, throwing her from the saddle. Somehow between getting back on her feet and capturing the skittish horse they became friends. Jane knew her parents would disapprove. All her life she'd been forbidden from mixing with local children. Lady Dorset said she didn't want her picking up bad habits from "ill-mannered, foul-mouthed peasants". But Jane had been lonely and Ferdinand was kind, so without discussing it they'd come to an understanding – their friendship would remain secret. As soon as they were in sight of Bradgate Hall, Ferdinand would ride behind Jane and when they reached the stables it was "miss" once more.

"King Edward is my cousin," she replied as they rode home. "He's nine, like me. We were born in the same month and I was named after his mother, Queen Jane, who died when he was only a week old."

"What's he like?"

"I don't really know. Last time I was at Richmond Palace I visited his chamber but as usual he wasn't well."

She thought of the sickly child with a pinched face surrounded by anxious physicians. His chamber was hung with the finest Flemish tapestries and he ate from cutlery encrusted with precious stones. Even his books were decorated with jewels. But he didn't look happy. He lay in his bed, swamped by his ornate coverlet, looking as if all he wanted was to be left in peace. Although he'd inherited the red hair and grey eyes of his father, it was impossible to picture him inspiring the same terror.

"Can you imagine being king at only nine years' old?" she said. "It would be awful."

"Why?" asked Ferdinand with a grin. "Palaces, banquets, jewels and more food than you can eat... It doesn't sound too bad."

"It's not like that," said Jane seriously. "When there's a child on the throne, the nobles always want his power. Even your own family can turn against you. Don't you know what happened to the last boy-king?"

Ferdinand shook his head.

"It was three kings before King Henry. That boy was also called Edward. He was thirteen when his father died but from the day he inherited the throne his uncle, Richard, was determined to take it from him. In the end

Richard shut Edward and his younger brother in the Tower of London and then he had them murdered."

"How?"

"One night his men smothered them with pillows while they were sleeping in their cell."

Ferdinand looked horrified.

"And you said King Edward isn't strong. Perhaps he won't live long. What if he should die? What would it mean for you?"

Even though they were in the middle of a snowy field, far from prying eyes, Jane glanced anxiously around her.

"Nothing, I hope."

"Really? Now that the old king's gone, how many people are there between you and the throne?"

Jane began counting on her fingers. "There are Edward's older sisters, Princess Mary and Princess Elizabeth."

"So that makes you third in line?"

Jane shook her head. "No, I'm not nearly as close as that. King Henry had an older sister called Margaret. Her granddaughter is Mary, Queen of Scots. She's only three years old but she's ahead of me."

"So that makes you fourth?"

"No. Mother's before me as well."

"So you're fifth."

"Fifth, yes," she agreed reluctantly.

"It's still close."

Jane nodded. It was certainly too close for comfort. "But," she pointed out, "they could all have children and then I would move further away. Even Mother's not too old to have a son."

"But what if they don't?" asked Ferdinand.

His concern sent a shiver down Jane's spine.

"I pray they do," she said quietly. "The last thing I want is to be queen."

"Miss Jane, where on earth have you been?" Mistress Ellen scurried across the courtyard towards the garden gate. "And look at you... The visitors are arriving and you're not fit to be seen."

Every Friday evening Lord and Lady Dorset invited noblemen and gentlefolk from the surrounding villages for supper. Most weeks there were at least fifty guests but sometimes the great hall was crowded with up to a hundred people, all in their finest clothes.

"Come this way and nobody will see you. Watch you don't get too much mud on the floor."

Jane pulled up her sopping hem and followed her nurse through a side door into the kitchen. It had four arched fireplaces, its walls were covered with gleaming copper pots, colanders, ladles and skimmers, and it was so hot and steamy Jane's freezing hands immediately began to tingle.

Stewed mutton, tongue pie, trout pasties, thick pea pottage, apple mousse and a prune tart were already laid out on a long trestle table in the centre of the room while scullery maids hurried from boiling cauldrons to spits of dripping meat, finishing off the last dishes.

"Eliza, run and get more honey and a jar of cloves," shouted Mrs Pipkin, the head cook, her ruddy face shining.

"Excuse us, excuse us," apologized Mistress Ellen as she and Jane dodged their way through the crowded room. They passed through a pantry lined with shelves of bottled fruit, flour, sugar, spices and salted meat and finally reached the servants' staircase. They hurried up it, emerging in a gloomy corridor close to Jane's room.

"Quick miss, put this on," Mistress Ellen held up a green silk robe with slashed sleeves and an exquisite taffeta lining.

"But that's my best dress. Mother reserves that for court."

"Well, she wants you to wear it tonight."

Jane was surprised. *I wonder why,* she thought as she pulled the gown over her red petticoats. Her nurse tugged at the bodice ties, hung a thick rope of pearls around her neck and then pinned Jane's auburn curls under a matching silk cap, taking more care than usual. *Mistress Ellen knows the reason!* she realized.

"What's going on?" she said. "Please tell me!"

Sometimes the old woman could be persuaded to gossip. She'd worked for the family all her life, first as a maid, then as Lady Dorset's nurse and now Jane's, and there was nothing she didn't know. But tonight she answered firmly, "I can't, Miss Jane. It's your mother's orders. Now let me see you."

If it was her mother's orders, Jane knew it was hopeless. Mistress Ellen was Lady Dorset's most loyal servant, and her eyes and ears at Bradgate Hall. As she turned around, her nurse's face crinkled in horror.

"Your bruise! We can't have that showing."

She began rubbing white paste onto Jane's face.

"Ow!" cried Jane, as the pressure made her cheek throb once more.

"Stop making a fuss," said Mistress Ellen crossly. "You provoked your mother, you know you did. Now let me add some colour."

She massaged red vermillion powder between her fingers, dabbed it on Jane's cheek and then studied her handiwork. "That's better. Now run along or Lady Dorset will be after me too."

Jane hurried down the passageway. From the hall she could hear the hubbub of conversation and the sounds of the minstrels' lutes and pipes. She turned a corner, bumped straight into her mother and dropped to her knees.

"Ah, there you are," said Lady Dorset crossly.

"I'm sorry if I kept you waiting. I ask for your blessing."

"Never mind all that. Get up and let me look at you."

Her mother inspected her carefully.

"What do you think?" she said at last, turning to her husband.

Lord Dorset was several inches shorter than his wife.

He had a fleshy face with a bulbous nose and he leaned heavily on a stick.

"She certainly looks the part," he answered. "Mistress Ellen has done well."

"Mistress Ellen?" snapped Lady Dorset. "What do you mean, Mistress Ellen? It's nothing to do with her. I chose the dress."

"Of course, Frances," said Lord Dorset hastily. "I meant *you've* done well. She looks..." He waved his hand, searching for the right word. "She looks regal. Just right for the announcement."

What announcement? thought Jane desperately.

"Father, excuse my impertinence, but please tell me what is happening," she said.

For once Lord Dorset didn't warn her to watch her manners and mind her own business. Instead he smiled triumphantly. "Just before he died, King Henry changed his will. He's disinherited Margaret."

"And along with her goes that brat Mary, Queen of Scots," added his wife.

"What does that mean?" asked Jane, already fearing the answer.

"It means you are now third in line to the throne."

"Third?" Jane was bewildered. Only an hour earlier she'd comforted herself that there were four people between her and the crown, but now at the stroke of the old king's quill there were just two. "Who are the others?" she asked.

"Princess Mary and Princess Elizabeth, of course," said her mother.

"What about you? Surely you're ahead of me?"

Lady Dorset frowned.

"Frances, it's no slight," said Lord Dorset comfortingly. "King Henry couldn't choose a married woman – that would be too much to expect – but just think, our Jane, only two from the throne. If we can't profit from that, we're fools. Now come along. Our guests are downstairs and I can't wait to tell them."

After consuming a plate of roast duck, partridge, and blackbird and sparrow pie, washed down with several goblets of sweet honey-coloured wine, Jane's father got unsteadily to his feet. He tapped the side of his glass with a silver knife and the company in the crowded hall fell silent.

"This is a special day in the Grey household," announced Lord Dorset, barely able to hide his glee at the family's good fortune. "In his wisdom, our late sovereign, King Henry VIII, has granted my daughter a great honour. In his last will, he has declared Jane third in line to the throne of England after the Princesses Mary and Elizabeth. Daughter, stand."

Jane rose awkwardly to her feet. She hated being the centre of attention. Occasionally, Lady Dorset insisted she accompany her on visits to the local villages. For these outings they donned their finest clothes and a trumpeter announced their presence in the market square. In no time butchers stopped skinning rabbits, blacksmiths' forges fell quiet and peddlers ceased shouting "ribbons", "lavender" and "hot-cross buns" and instead stared curiously at the grand folk who had come calling. Jane always felt uncomfortable but her mother loved it and regally scattered pennies.

"Stop being so pathetic," hissed Lady Dorset. "You're blushing like a baby."

Jane blushed even more.

"All right, sit," whispered her mother a moment later. "Enough showing off."

Jane sank onto the bench, feeling wretched. It was so unfair; whatever she did was wrong.

As she sat down, her father leaned over. "Frances, we should celebrate. How about a round of cards? I feel my luck's in." He chuckled. "Sir Howarth's over there. We might take him for a couple of pounds."

Lady Dorset shook her head.

"I have more important things on my mind."

"Like what?"

"Rearranging our trip to London. Jane must come with us now, of course."

Jane's heart sank. For the past few days, every time she was scolded or beaten, her one comfort had been that her parents would soon be leaving Bradgate Hall. From Christmas until Lent, the court was a social whirl of masked balls, jousts and banquets as courtiers flitted between the sumptuous palaces of Greenwich, Whitehall, Westminster and Richmond. As a Lady of the Queen's Privy Chamber, Lady Dorset would be much in demand, particularly as she'd already missed the first month of the season waiting for the birth of a niece.

"Why should she come?" said her father.

He was a man who liked his routine. At Bradgate Hall his day never varied. A breakfast of salted herring and beer at seven o'clock, hawking until noon, a light lunch followed by a visit to a neighbour, supper at six and then he retired to his chamber as the clock struck ten.

"Because the situation has altered," answered Lady Dorset irritably. "We must show her off a little. The new king's coronation is the perfect time."

Jane was horrified. At least at Bradgate Hall she could get away from her parents; in fact, they seemed positively allergic to her company. Lady Dorset arranged for her day to be filled with bracing rides in the park and hours of lessons. Every morning apart from Sunday she studied Latin, Greek, Italian and French, as well as the Bible and music. Her tutor, Doctor Harding, was a gentle schoolmaster with a lilting voice and infinite patience, and Jane enjoyed her lessons, but it was her daily rides with Ferdinand that she would miss most. At court she would have to trail after her parents, and she would never have a moment to herself. Then there were the endless, complicated rules and traditions that meant that somehow, despite trying not to, she always caused offence. Her mother would scold her for curtseying at the wrong time, or addressing a lord with the wrong title. It was all so difficult. But here, riding on the moors, she was free.

"Having Jane with us will be such a bore," moaned Lord Dorset.

"I know, but we're in great need of money."

Jane's parents spent lavish sums on clothes, jewels, horses and paintings, and frequently lost large sums gambling. Despite owning acres of land, they were constantly in debt. *But now*, Jane thought bitterly, *they have something valuable to sell – me.*

As the great-niece of King Henry, Jane was already a catch. Many times she'd heard Mistress Ellen gossiping with the maids about which fine gentleman she might marry and how big her marriage settlement could be. But with the old king's will there was now a much greater prize – the throne of England and Wales. If the cards fell a certain way, it would be hers, and her parents were clearly determined to make the most of it.

"You are cunning, Frances," said Lord Dorset with frank admiration. "Take Jane with us... Good idea. But everything's packed. We can't delay things now."

"Don't fuss. Mistress Ellen will arrange everything. Jane, go and tell your nurse you must both be ready to leave for London straight after breakfast. We're off at seven o'clock sharp."

Jane knew there was no point arguing or pleading; she must do as she was told, or risk another beating. She curtsied and hurried to her chamber.

Mistress Ellen was sound asleep on the trundle cot at the foot of Jane's bed when Jane gently shook her shoulder and told her Lady Dorset's orders. The old woman sat bolt upright.

"Right, miss. Let's get on with it," she said. "There's much to be done and your mother can't stand to be kept waiting."

6

"*At* last," said Lady Dorset as they trotted over the brow of a hill. "Henry, do you see it?"

Lord Dorset shaded his eyes from the low winter sun. Ahead was a great stone ruin with tumbledown walls, and beyond it were meadows, but then, in the distance, a collection of towers and steeples clustered beside a wide river – London.

Jane and her parents had spent a week riding sedately south from Leicestershire. They were a party of ten – the Dorsets, Mistress Ellen, two manservants and four grooms – followed by a lumbering wagon laden with trunks.

Each night they had stayed at one of the grand houses along the route, as Lord and Lady Dorset visited their wealthy friends.

On the road they had passed travelling minstrels, beggars and every kind of peddler, and south of Hatfield there had been such a downpour that the track turned into a muddy bog. But it was the monasteries that had made the greatest impression on Jane. Outside every town and village were abandoned priories and convents, their doors kicked in, their colourful glass windows smashed and the lead stolen from their roofs.

"Good riddance," muttered Lord Dorset as they trotted past the dismal ruin. "Corrupt places full of lazy charlatans. Best thing King Henry ever did was to close them down. No more worshipping daft relics. No more rosary beads and all that Latin mumbo-jumbo. At least now, when I go to church, I can understand what the parson is saying."

His wife laughed.

"Henry, we all know you're a true believer in the new religion, but don't pretend the king was too. He only did it so he could get his hands on Anne Boleyn."

Jane, riding just behind her parents, was stunned. Anne Boleyn's name was never, ever mentioned in public. It was only by eavesdropping on servants or badgering Mistress Ellen that Jane had learned anything of the old king's most scandalous wife. King Henry was already married when he'd fallen under Anne's spell. It was not long before she'd convinced him to divorce his first wife and marry her instead. But there was a problem. The king needed the permission of the Pope to divorce, and the Pope wouldn't give it. So one day Henry outlawed the Catholic Church, made himself head of a new Church of England and married his mistress. "He had to do it because she was pregnant," Mistress Ellen had told Jane. "But although she got her crown, she didn't keep it for long. The king soon tired of her and had her executed. But he must feel bad about it now, for woe betide anyone who mentions her name."

And yet here was her mother, happily gossiping when any of the servants might overhear. *Now the king is dead,* thought Jane, *I suppose he doesn't need minding any more.* But it felt strange, hearing the forbidden words.

"That's not true, Frances," said Lord Dorset irritably. "Once Anne was killed, Henry could have crawled back to Rome. He chose to stay a new-religionist because he believed in it."

"Crawling was hardly his style," scoffed Lady Dorset. "No, he needed the old church's money... And he got it. Look at this place. It's been well and truly looted."

Jane saw that all that remained of the huge priory was a bell tower, a few buttresses and a graveyard overgrown with nettles. It made her shudder.

The party trotted on towards a small village.

"This is as good a place as any to rest," declared Lord Dorset. "We'll water the horses here and eat at the inn."

"Is there time?" His wife frowned. "I don't want to be shut out of the city for the night."

"Of course there is. We'll get there well before the curfew. You'll see."

The landlady was a thin woman with sharp elbows and a greedy smile. At the sight of prosperous customers she bustled over shouting, "Paul, clear the parlour," and then, "Sir, madam, let me take your things."

Lord Dorset struggled out of his velvet doublet while his wife and Jane took off their fur-lined coats and hats.

"Make sure no one touches our things," ordered Lady Dorset. "I don't want them getting dirty."

The landlady smiled obsequiously. "Of course, madam. Now, what can I get you? We've pigeon pie or mutton stew and I've a very fine bottle of wine."

"Wine sounds excellent and pie for three," said Lord Dorset. "And take some broth to the servants."

"Very good, sir. Come this way. You can have a bit of peace and quiet in here."

They crossed the crowded tavern and entered a poky room with a sagging ceiling, a rickety pine table, two benches and a smoking fire.

Lady Dorset wiped the seat with her handkerchief before sitting down.

"So, Henry, who's your favourite?" she asked, pulling off her kid gloves.

Inwardly Jane groaned; the entire journey her parents had been working their way through lists of the most eligible bachelors in the land.

"Cumberland's son," said her father.

"Don't be silly; he's too young. Jane could almost be his mother."

"What about the Earl of Wessex?"

"The family's not nearly rich enough. They couldn't afford her. A thousand pounds is all they'd be good for."

"How much do you think we could get?"

"At least half as much again. Maybe more. Enough to keep Bradgate Hall going for a couple of years."

"Then how about Arundel's boy? They're as rich as Croesus."

Lady Dorset pursued her lips.

"They are, but you know what Sir John's like. The old man's too mean to pay, not with two princesses standing between her and the throne."

"I suppose you're right," said Lord Dorset dejectedly. "Perhaps we're being too hasty. King Edward's health is bad, Mary's a Catholic and everyone knows Elizabeth's a bastard. We could be better off waiting, particularly if Edward falls ill. We might get more for her later."

"No," said his wife dismissively. "The king is getting stronger and what if one of the princesses marries? There'll be babies on the way and Jane's value will plummet. We should move now to get the biggest marriage settlement. Unless..."

Her eyes brightened.

"Unless what, my dear?" asked Lord Dorset.

Just then the landlady came in with a flagon of wine and three pies.

"We'll discuss it later," said Lady Dorset as the woman set the food on the table. "Now eat up. We can't be late."

After a hurried grace, Jane picked up her spoon, but she was no longer hungry. Her mother was looking too pleased with herself and she had to find out why.

After lunch, the party set off on the last leg of their long journey south. The rutted track descended gently through grassy meadows and ploughed fields. As they got closer to London, they passed windmills, their sails turning in the gentle breeze, lines of flapping laundry and colourful bolts of cloth the size of carpets drying on tenterhooks in the afternoon sun.

The road was busier now, and lumbering carts laden with honking geese and grunting pigs heading to market forced them to slow their horses.

"Tell them to get out of our way," Lady Dorset ordered one of the grooms.

But it was impossible for the cumbersome wagons to move quickly to one side.

"Henry, I told you we'd be late," she snapped. "We should never have stopped for lunch."

By the time they finally reached Lud Gate, the most westerly entrance in the city walls, the church bells were tolling five o'clock and Jane had spent almost nine hours in the saddle.

"Hurry!" called the gatekeeper. "I'll be locking up at dusk."

Lud Gate doubled as a prison. Hanging from its parapet were three bodies, their entrails dangling. Jane quickly looked away but she couldn't avoid seeing the cripples in filthy rags begging for a last coin before being herded out of the city for the night.

After tipping the gatekeeper a penny, the Dorsets passed through the ancient walls. St Paul's Cathedral loomed ahead, its medieval steeple towering into the sky.

In the fading light, they rode the length of the cathedral and then on to Cheapside, a broad cobbled street with grand buildings and hundreds of shops and stalls. Apothecaries displayed herbs, spices and potions in coloured jars. Carcasses of pigs, cows and sheep hung from butchers' hooks. Jewellers sat at their tables weighing nuggets of gold and silver. Bolts of rich cloth filled the tailors' windows and everywhere there were trestle tables and baskets piled high with cabbages, carrots, apples, rounds of cheddar, lavender, oysters and salt.

Despite her weariness, Jane was excited by the bustling scene.

"What's that?" she asked, pointing at a great stone building with glass windows and an arched entrance from which boys in blue smocks were tumbling out.

"That's the Mercers' Hall, miss," answered Mistress Ellen. "They import wool. They're the richest guild in London and the boys are their apprentices. I suppose they're all off to enjoy themselves before the curfew."

The guilds controlled all trade in the city. There were

guilds for bakers, drapers, masons, glaziers, ironmongers, goldsmiths and vintners, and every year each guild took on around fifty boys to train in their chosen profession.

Jane soon spotted another impressive hall painted with a coat of arms made up of tools and rafters.

"Is that the Carpenters' Guild?" she asked Mistress Ellen.

"Yes, miss, and opposite there's the Clothworkers and the Pewterers' Hall."

Jane looked enviously at the jolly, chattering boys in blue, but soon the road became narrower and stone facades gave way to crowded timber houses. Several times the Dorsets had to stop to allow a swineherd to round up his snuffling pigs or a farmer his flock of sheep, and the stench of sewage was so strong Jane pulled her cape over her nose.

"This is revolting," moaned Lady Dorset. "Will we ever get there?"

Finally, just as the sun was setting, they left the crowded alleys behind and rode into a large grassy field. On the far side was a scaffold and beyond that their destination – the Tower of London.

They pulled up the horses close by the banks of the castle's muddy moat and Jane jumped to the ground. Her legs and shoulders were stiff and it felt strange to be walking after such a long ride. Gratefully she handed her reins to one of the grooms and then followed her parents across a wooden drawbridge towards Lyon Tower, the main entrance to the fort, with Mistress Ellen following close behind.

They were halfway across the bridge when the curfew bells began to clang, warning that everyone must stay indoors until morning.

"You're the last in today," said a limping warden as a huge iron portcullis rattled down behind them. "Follow me and I'll show you to your quarters."

He held up a lamp and led them along a shadowy road, paved with flint, that ran between two high slate walls.

"I don't like it here. It's so dark," whispered Mistress Ellen as she hobbled along. "I wish we could stay at Greenwich Palace instead."

It was Jane's first visit to the Tower and she felt the same way. Most of the ancient fortress was used as a jail but it was traditional for the king and his court to lodge here for the week before the coronation, so they had no choice.

"Get changed quickly, Jane," said Lady Dorset when they reached their draughty rooms in Beauchamp Tower. "Supper is in an hour. It'll be served in the Great Hall."

"We're banqueting tonight?" Jane was dismayed; all she wanted was to collapse on the bed and sleep.

"Of course. We must make the most of every opportunity. Now pull yourself together."

Mistress Ellen heaved herself from a stool and opened one of the leather trunks that had just been delivered to the room.

"What would you like her to wear, madam?"

Lady Dorset studied her daughter critically. "You're so sallow and short, and that awful frizzy hair... and don't frown all the time. Nobody likes a girl that's glum."

Jane had been told many times that her looks were a disappointment, but her mother's words still hurt.

"I suppose the mauve damask might give you a bit of colour," sighed Lady Dorset, "with the lilac underskirt and cork wedges on your shoes to give you height. And Mistress Ellen, one long plait and no jewellery. I want Jane to look modest, not like some of the trollops we'll see tonight."

Mistress Ellen set to work at once. She scrubbed Jane's face, neck and hands, changed her linen smock, tightened the drawstrings on her corset, pulled on the dress and lastly attached blocks to Jane's heels and toes.

"Well, miss, that's the best I can do," she said. "Don't provoke your mother and mind you behave."

The Great Hall was enormous, with a high-beamed ceiling, walls painted with flowers and a roaring fire. Down its centre was a long oak table set with silver candlesticks, gilt plates, Venetian glasses, and vases of red and white roses – the emblem of the Tudor kings.

"Lord and Lady Dorset and their daughter, the Lady Jane Grey," announced the Chamberlain in a booming voice and then a chubby serving boy led them through the crowded hall to their seats.

Jane was used to her mother's elaborate wardrobe but as they wove their way through the teeming hall she was dazzled by the courtiers' clothes. The ladies' bodices were cut indecently low, gowns slashed to display embroidered underskirts twinkling with gemstones, and their hair was fashionably crimped and curled. She stumbled, almost falling to the ground. *Concentrate*, she told herself. *Mother will never forgive you if you embarrass her here.*

As they reached the centre of the long table the serving boy pointed to a bench just three places to the left of a high-backed chair – the king's seat – and bowed.

Lady Dorset ran her eyes along the table, calculating. The king, his regent and then her... Yes, all correct and in order.

"Lady Jane Grey, please follow me," said the boy.

Balancing precariously on her unsteady shoes, Jane went all the way round the far end of the table and back until she was opposite her parents.

"There, my lady," he said, just as the heralds sounded a loud trumpet salute and the double doors at the far end of the chamber were thrown open.

In walked King Edward. He was dressed in a doublet of purple velvet with solid gold buttons and from his belt hung a glittering dagger. But, for all his finery, he looked delicate, nervous and very young.

Slowly he paraded along the hall, courtiers bowing and curtseying as he passed, followed by a stout middle-aged woman and a young girl of around fourteen.

The older woman, Jane recognized immediately. It was Princess Mary, King Henry's eldest daughter by his first wife, the Spanish Queen Catherine of Aragon. She was dressed in an ill-fitting, frumpy dark gown, her skin was blotchy, her lips thin and colourless, and she squinted short-sightedly. In her hand she clutched a chain of heavy gold beads, proof she was a recusant – a Catholic who refused to convert to the new faith. Jane was simultaneously fascinated and repulsed. She'd been taught that Catholics were dangerously mistaken in their beliefs. They were deceitful and false; their first loyalty was to the Pope rather than king and country. And now here, only feet away from her, was the most famous Catholic in the land, flaunting her rosary beads. Jane couldn't remember exactly what her father objected to about Catholics – something to do with encouraging the worship of Jesus's mother rather than God. But she knew they were wrong. Yet Princess Mary seemed unashamed.

The girl behind her was quite different. Whereas Mary looked worn and tired, she was young and fresh, dressed in a demure white gown, her red hair tied back with a ribbon. The simplicity of her dress highlighted her rosy cheeks and jet-black eyes. *She must be Elizabeth*, thought Jane. She'd never met this cousin. For years the princess had been banished from court because, it was rumoured, her coal-black eyes reminded King Henry too much of her disgraced mother, Anne Boleyn. And then Jane remembered that Queen Anne had been imprisoned and beheaded right here in the Tower. She shuddered. What must it be like for Elizabeth to visit the very place where her mother had been killed?

At last the king reached his chair but the princesses walked on, around the head of the banqueting table and back along Jane's side. They came closer and closer and Jane realized that she was going to be sitting between them. She was within a few feet of the three people who stood between her and the throne.

"God save the king," boomed the Chamberlain.

"To the king's health," replied the company as one voice, "and that of his sisters, Princesses Mary and Elizabeth."

And no one in the room meant it more sincerely than Jane.

8

"You're to go straight to the king's rooms, miss," ordered Mistress Ellen.

Jane was surprised. After last night's banquet her mother had been furious. Why was she always so timid and shy? What a fool she'd looked in front of the whole court! Why, she'd hardly said a word to the princesses! How could she expect to secure a great marriage when she acted more like the village idiot than a lady? Jane tried to explain that neither Elizabeth nor Mary had spoken to her, but her mother was having none of it. She'd ordered Jane to stay out of sight, rather to Jane's relief, and yet here she was, being summoned by the king.

"What's going on?" she asked, putting down her book.

"I don't know, miss, but hurry. You must not keep him waiting."

Moments later they entered a grand room hung with scarlet and gold brocade. The tiny king was seated on an upright chair between two men, one tall with a straggling beard and a high stiff ruff, the other handsome, with merry eyes and a cap sewn with ostrich feathers.

Her nurse poked her and Jane curtseyed, more mystified than ever.

"So, Lord Dorset, this is your daughter?" said the dashing man.

Jane's parents were standing by the window, either side of an elegant, fair-haired woman in a French hood and a black damask kirtle, her only ornament a simple gold cross on a chain.

"Indeed it is, Lord Admiral."

"She's a plain little thing, wouldn't you say?"

"Plain but healthy, sir," answered Lord Dorset, "and she's a faithful new-religionist, brought up with a firm hand by her mother. She knows what's expected of her."

"And you say she's an excellent scholar?" continued the man her father called "Lord Admiral".

"Certainly, sir. Her tutor tells me he's never had a finer student. She's fluent in French and Italian, and her Greek and Latin are excellent."

"Then perhaps Lady Jane would spend an afternoon with me," ventured Edward in a surprisingly high voice. "We could do a translation together."

The tall man squeezed the young king's shoulder, and immediately the boy turned to him and added, "If you think that's a good idea, Uncle."

"I'll consider it."

Jane felt sorry for the boy-king, so powerless he couldn't even invite his cousin to his rooms without checking with someone first. And then she remembered her mother's angry words – *Why was she always so timid?* Here was a chance to be kind and show courage, so she curtseyed and said, "Your Majesty, my nurse could fetch one of my translations, if you'd like."

The words were hardly out of her mouth before Lady Dorset pulled her to her knees.

"Your Grace, please forgive our daughter," apologized her father. "She should know never to address the king directly unless first spoken to."

Jane's heart sank. She'd done the wrong thing again and no doubt she would pay for it.

"Mistress Ellen, take Jane to her rooms. I will deal with her shortly," snapped Lady Dorset as soon as they were outside the king's apartment.

Jane followed her nurse forlornly up the spiral staircase of the Beauchamp Tower.

"Miss, what were you thinking?" asked Mistress Ellen. "Your mother is furious and I don't blame her."

Wearily, Jane sat down on a stool.

"I only wanted to be nice to Edward. He looked so crushed by those men."

"Those men?" tutted her nurse. "Do you have any idea who they are?"

Jane shook her head.

"They're the king's uncles. The one with the beard is the Duke of Somerset. He'll rule until King Edward is grown so you can't go upsetting him."

"And the other?"

Mistress Ellen's wrinkled face broke into a smile. "Oh,

now he's a catch, miss. Sir Thomas Seymour is his name. He's said to be the handsomest bachelor at court. He's also the Lord Admiral of the Fleet but I've heard that's not enough for him. He's madly envious of his brother." She leaned closer and whispered, "There's a rumour that Princess Elizabeth turned him down so he's proposed to Queen Katherine instead."

"That can't be right," said Jane. "She's only been widowed three weeks."

"If you believe the gossip, miss, she loved Sir Thomas long before King Henry picked her as his queen. Now she's free and wealthy enough to do as she pleases, and you must admit she's beautiful."

"I've never seen her," said Jane.

"Yes you have, miss. She was there this afternoon. King Edward is her stepson and she's fond of him so she attends every important meeting."

Jane remembered the tall fair-haired woman standing between her parents.

"My visit wasn't important, was it?"

"It might have been."

"How?"

Mistress Ellen nudged her charge. "Miss, for all that book work, you are a fool. Your parents are planning a royal marriage. What do you think of that?"

Jane didn't answer – she'd long ago learned that anything she said to Mistress Ellen went straight to her mother – but her mind whirred. Her marry King

Edward... So this was what her mother had been planning over lunch at the inn!

"I said, what do you think?" asked her nurse, studying her carefully.

Before Jane had time to think of a suitable answer, the door was thrown open and in walked Lady Dorset.

"After all my work," she thundered. "After all the hours your father and I have spent getting you an audience with the Seymours, this is how you repay us. By talking to the king... You idiot! You could have ruined everything." From behind her back she pulled a birch switch. "Perhaps this will help you remember your manners."

Jane flinched. Being whipped was excruciatingly painful and left her unable to sit for days. Instinctively she backed away, but her mother was too quick for her. She grabbed Jane's arm, flung her onto the bed and slammed down the cane. Jane cried out as the whip swished again and again, tearing into her back and thighs.

"Madam, the coronation's tomorrow," implored Mistress Ellen. "Nothing around the face, madam. Nothing that will show."

Lady Dorset ignored the nurse and lashed out again – a smarting blow on Jane's arm – and then abruptly stopped. Jane pulled herself up from the quilt, relieved the beating was over so quickly, and saw a young page standing in the open doorway.

"Well, what is it?" asked Lady Dorset irritably.

"I have a message for Lady Jane Grey," stammered the

boy, obviously shaken by the scene he'd stumbled upon. "She is to come to the dowager queen's rooms directly after his Majesty's coronation. And she is to come alone."

"Alone?" said Lady Dorset. "Why?"

The page blushed. "I don't know, madam."

"I wonder what that's about," mused Lady Dorset once the boy had left. "Mistress Ellen, I don't care what Katherine says, you will accompany my daughter and report back every word."

"Yes, madam," said the nurse.

"Now, where was I?" And Jane's mother picked up the birch once more.

Jane waited with Mistress Ellen outside an ornate wooden door guarded by soldiers – the entrance to the dowager queen's apartment. To pass the time and stop herself from becoming too nervous, she thought over the events of the past two extraordinary days.

On Saturday she had joined the king's coronation parade through London. The courtiers were dressed in their finest clothes, the streets were swept and freshly gravelled, and every window was hung with tapestries and carpets. Along the way she saw fountains spraying jets of wine, plays and pageants, choirs, and even a tightrope walker descending from the spire of St Paul's Cathedral.

After spending a night at Westminster Palace, the court travelled to Whitehall in barges garlanded with flowers and then walked the last few steps to Westminster Abbey.

Jane had never seen such a magnificent building. The church had huge arches, columns and pillars, and before the ancient altar was a throne covered in gold brocade.

King Edward wore a white suit embroidered with rubies, diamonds and pearls that twinkled in the candlelight. He was lifted onto his throne by his uncle, the Duke of Somerset. He looked tiny and nervous, and as the long service dragged on, Jane felt sorry for him, despite all the splendour.

One of the guards interrupted her thoughts. "The dowager queen will see you now." He frowned. "But your nurse is not required."

"Lady Jane never goes anywhere without me," protested Mistress Ellen.

"Madam, these are the dowager queen's express instructions," answered the soldier firmly. "Lady Jane, please follow me."

More curious than ever, Jane entered a comfortable parlour with a wool carpet, oak panelling, and shelves and shelves of books. Katherine was sitting on a stool near the fire. Her fashionably pale skin was accentuated by her rouged mouth and she wore a grey mourning gown nipped in to highlight her tiny waist, a matching headdress that hid most of her fair hair and the same simple gold chain that Jane had noticed in the king's chamber.

Katherine rose gracefully to her feet and kissed Jane warmly on both cheeks.

"I thought it was time we met properly – and without anyone else present. I hope that's all right with you?"

"Of course, your Highness."

"Good, then come and sit by the fire."

She patted a chair. For a moment Jane didn't know what to do. Her back and legs were not yet healed from her whipping but if she stayed standing Katherine would be bound to ask why and it was too humiliating to explain.

She lowered herself gingerly into the chair, trying not to wince.

The dowager queen leaned forward. "My dear, are you happy at Bradgate Hall?" She spoke gently and with such a kindly expression that Jane didn't know how to answer. "You are a sensitive girl. It was good of you to offer to send the king work and unfair that you were punished for it."

The page boy! thought Jane. *He had told his mistress what he'd seen.*

"A girl of your age can sometimes do well lodging away from home," Katherine went on carefully. "I'm shortly to move to Dormer Palace in Chelsea. It's a charming house – quiet but well situated by the river. Would you come and stay?"

Jane couldn't believe her ears. Girls were often placed in grand families, where they waited on their hostess and in return were taught music, dancing and social polish, enhancing their chance of a good marriage. Jane knew many people had requested her but so far Lady Dorset had always refused – none was impressive enough for her daughter. *But Katherine is the first lady in the land*, thought Jane excitedly. *Mother will not be able to object.*

"I would be honoured, your Highness," she said, beaming.

"Good. In that case I will speak to Lady Dorset first thing in the morning. Dormer Palace is currently being refurbished but it should be ready by the end of Lent. If it is all right with your mother, you may join me then."

"**Remember**, Miss Jane, if Lady Dorset hears of any mishaps, you'll be straight back to Bradgate Hall."

Over the past few months, Mistress Ellen had said this a hundred times. Jane must do as she was told, upset no one and write home frequently reporting anything of interest. Her parents had said exactly the same thing when they learned of Katherine's invitation. It was a golden opportunity. The dowager queen was influential and while the Duke of Somerset wasn't keen on a marriage between Jane and Edward, the Lord Admiral was, and now that he was married to Katherine there was hope. Surely a fond stepmother and a favourite uncle could between them plant the idea in the boy-king's head. Lady Dorset had grudgingly admitted that Jane had done well. A summer in Chelsea was just what was required.

"That must be the palace, miss," said Ferdinand, who was accompanying Jane and her nurse on the long journey south. His horse was several paces ahead and he was pointing at a red-brick manor.

Jane halted her mare and gazed at her new home. Dormer Palace was not large but it was a handsome building, set in the middle of pretty gardens planted with cherry trees, roses and privet hedges with a large lawn running down to a bend in the River Thames.

"It's beautiful," she said.

By the time they reached the gravel courtyard, Katherine and Sir Thomas Seymour were waiting for them, along with several excitable greyhounds. Since her marriage, the dowager queen had dispensed with mourning clothes and instead wore a crimson dress with wide sleeves and an underskirt richly worked in gold.

"Welcome," she said, smiling warmly as the dogs yapped around her ankles. She picked up the smallest, a thin short-haired puppy.

"Calm down, Boxer! Jane, are you tired after your long journey?"

"No, your Highness," Jane answered, climbing down from her horse. "I'm fine, thank you."

"Not 'your Highness'," corrected the dowager queen. "Remember, this is now your home. You must call me Katherine. Tell me, who is with you?"

Briefly, Jane introduced Mistress Ellen and Ferdinand.

"Ferdinand – that's an unusual name," commented Sir Thomas.

"My mother is from Spain, sir," explained Ferdinand.

"Ever been there?"

"No, sir."

"Good. They're all papists. Now, why don't you and Mistress Ellen both go to the kitchen and find yourselves a mug of beer. Jane, come with us."

From the corner of her eye, Jane watched Ferdinand disappear into the servants' entrance. He was the one person she would miss from Bradgate Hall, yet because he was only a groom she couldn't even say goodbye properly. But at least, she consoled herself, they'd spent the past few days together.

The journey from Leicestershire to Chelsea had taken over a week. Each night they'd stayed at inns along the way and once Mistress Ellen retired to bed, Jane had crept down to the stable yard to find Ferdinand and they had chatted until the spring moon was high in the sky. They had talked of home and Jane's future, but what she had enjoyed most was listening to Ferdinand's plans. For as long as he could remember, he'd known exactly what he wanted to be – a carpenter. He was now twelve years' old and had his heart set on becoming an apprentice in London.

"How will you persuade the guild to take you on?" Jane had asked one evening. "There must be hundreds of boys wanting to join."

From a linen sack Ferdinand pulled a small box. Inside were white and black wooden figures, each no larger than a finger. Jane picked one up. They were chess pieces, with tiny clothes, crowns, swords and even a little drawbridge for the castle.

"I carved them," said Ferdinand.

Jane examined each piece carefully. "They're fantastic. If these don't convince the guild, nothing will."

"I've decided to go and see them on the way back to Leicestershire. No one at Bradgate Hall will know if I make a detour to London."

And now, Jane thought sadly as she followed the Lord Admiral into Dormer Palace, she wouldn't hear for months whether Ferdinand was to be an apprentice or not. She could hardly send a letter to a mere groom, and even if she did, what was the point? Ferdinand couldn't read.

"We have a surprise for you," said the Lord Admiral as they entered a flag-stoned hall. There were several large oil paintings on the walls and a squawking parrot caged in the corner. "Look who's here."

Standing by the fireplace was a red-headed girl. As she turned around, Jane's heart sank. It was Elizabeth. Jane hadn't seen her since the banquet on the eve of the king's coronation when the haughty princess had not said a word to her.

"A curtsey is polite," said Elizabeth after a long pause.

"I'm sorry, ma'am," stammered Jane, blushing and dropping to the ground.

"Not 'ma'am'," the girl corrected. "It's 'your Highness'."

Jane coloured once more.

"I'm sorry, your Highness."

"I've told Princess Elizabeth that she may stay as long as she likes," said Katherine. "You will do your lessons together. I'm sure it will make them more pleasant for both of you."

Jane was not as confident, and she knew that she must find a way not to aggravate the proud princess if she was to enjoy her time away from Bradgate Hall.

Jane soon settled into a comfortable routine at Dormer Palace. In the morning she studied with Elizabeth and their tutor, John Aylmer. Mr Aylmer was exacting but although the lessons were difficult Jane enjoyed them, and soon learned to keep her mouth shut if she knew an answer and her prickly cousin did not.

As soon as lessons were over the princess disappeared but Jane wasn't lonely. She walked the greyhounds in the beautiful gardens and nearby woods, took a rowboat upstream, fed the parrot in the great hall or sewed with Katherine in the parlour.

In the evening the Lord Admiral joined them all for supper. Often he looked strained and distracted. He had fallen from favour at court because his brother, the Duke of Somerset, was furious with him for marrying the dowager queen. A kind word from his wife, however, would lift his spirits, and before long he would cheerfully tease them all, especially Elizabeth, who glowed in his company.

Jane had never felt so welcome and, to add to her happiness, a week after she arrived Katherine sent Mistress Ellen back to Leicestershire, saying that Jane was too old for a nurse and that she would find her a suitable maid instead.

"Would you mind taking Boxer out?" Katherine asked one summer afternoon. "He seems restless."

Jane put down her embroidery. Sunlight was streaming through the windows. Cheerfully she picked up the puppy and carried him into the gardens.

The roses were blooming, bees hovered over the lavender and the air was heavy with the scent of thyme, jasmine and honeysuckle.

"Let's go to the river," she said, setting Boxer down.

Excitedly, the dog dashed this way and that. When they reached the water Jane sat down in the shade of a willow tree, but she hadn't been resting long when Boxer came bounding over with a mossy stick in his mouth. She tossed it along the bank and moments later he scampered back. She threw it again and the puppy soon came back, his pink tongue dripping.

"You need to cool off," said Jane, rubbing Boxer's ears affectionately. "You're even hotter than I am. Let's go to the woods."

To the west of the garden was a pretty forest. Jane chose a path through dappled trees. It was so cool and pleasant that she went further than usual and arrived at an unfamiliar fork in the trail. She chose the narrower, shadier path, trampling over brambles and long grass until the trail dipped into a hollow, where she was surprised to see a small, dilapidated stone building.

She climbed down a steep path to a tiny chapel with a porch, arched windows and a tiled roof with an iron cross all overgrown with ivy. Curiously, she approached the portico. The rotten door was ajar. She stopped. Inside someone was chanting. *Why hold a service in such an out of the way place?* she wondered.

She picked Boxer up, gently holding his muzzle to keep him quiet and peeked through the door. Inside a group of people were facing an altar and an old man, dressed in a white cassock with a purple hat, was swinging an urn of burning incense and reading a sermon ... in Latin. Catholics!

Heart pumping, Jane crept away and only when she was certain she was hidden by the dense trees did she run home as fast as her elaborate dress would allow.

She burst into the dowager queen's parlour.

"Recusants!" she said breathlessly. "They're holding a mass in the forest."

Katherine dropped her quill. "Are you sure?" she asked, instinctively touching her gold cross.

"I'm certain."

In no time the dowager queen found her husband. The Lord Admiral summoned his men and Jane led the way through the wood to the gloomy hollow.

"Come out, traitors! You're under arrest," shouted Sir Thomas.

Eight worshippers shuffled out of the tiny chapel. There were six women, nervously crossing themselves, a limping priest and a pale young man with a beaky nose and a coat tied with string. Jane hardly dared look at them. They were traitors, worse than vermin, her father said.

"Please sir, let us go," begged a shabby woman with tears in her eyes. "We weren't doing any harm."

"Not doing any harm?" said Sir Thomas incredulously. "You know very well the king has banned this dangerous nonsense."

"Sir, all we want is to worship the Lord in our own way," pleaded the woman. "Can't we be left in peace to do that?"

Several others began to weep. "Have pity on us, sir. We've children to feed. What will become of them without us?"

"You should have thought of that earlier."

The younger man cleared his throat. "Please sir, let the women go. Take me instead."

"And who are you?" asked Sir Thomas.

"My name is John Hawker."

"You're not from around here are you?"

The man shook his head and pointed to a basket of ribbons. "No sir. I'm a peddler. I travel the country."

"Then perhaps you don't know that I am Sir Thomas Seymour," said the Lord Admiral. "As an uncle of the king, I cannot flout the law. You will all be locked up for two months, except the priest. He gets a year. Men, take them away."

The bedraggled party were led off.

"That was a bit of luck," said Sir Thomas cheerfully as the last one shuffled away. "The king loves hearing of Catholics being rounded up. I could soon be back in favour. Now shall we go home?"

"You go ahead and deal with them," replied his wife. "I want to see their church. Jane, would you like to come?"

Jane was surprised to find she would. Now that the Catholics were gone, she was curious to know exactly what these sinful people got up to.

Together she and Katherine pushed open the crumbling door. Jane wasn't sure what she'd expected, but she found herself in a simple church with four pillars and a few pews riddled with woodworm. The altar was also surprisingly bare. She'd heard tales of Catholics hoarding collections of gold, relics and paintings of saints but here there was just a rough trestle table covered with a linen cloth, and on it a small loaf of bread and a jug of wine. Apart from the smoky incense it was as plain as the chapel Jane attended each day. But Katherine shook her head.

"When will they ever learn?" She picked up the bread. "No doubt that charlatan priest claimed he'd transform this into Christ's flesh." She sighed. "People will believe anything. Take it and leave it for the birds. It will do more good there."

Jane was scraping up the last of the crumbs – when she noticed, sticking out just an inch beyond the tablecloth, a smooth piece of pale wood. She stared at it. It was shaped like the tip of a clog. And then it moved, ever so slightly. She gasped. It *was* a clog and in it was a foot. Another traitor was under the table, only inches away!

Silently, Jane tugged at Katherine's sleeve.

"What is it?" asked the dowager queen.

"There's another one here," she whispered. "Under the altar."

Katherine's eyes opened wide but her voice was calm and firm as she marched across the church calling, "Come out. You've been found."

There was no response.

"I said, come out." The dowager queen poked the tablecloth.

The clog shuffled towards them ... followed by a thin ankle ... and a skirt.

"Why, it's a girl!" exclaimed the dowager queen, much to Jane's relief.

The child got slowly to her feet. She was slim with dark wavy hair, a round face and solemn green eyes. Her linen dress was patched and shabby but her white collar and cap were clean.

"What's your name?" asked Katherine.

"Maud Scythe, your Highness." The girl curtseyed respectfully.

"I haven't seen you in the village."

"No, your Highness," said the girl in a lilting West Country accent.

"Then how do you know who I am?"

"The woman I was travelling with told me. She was going to bring me to your house, but first she said she had something to do. I never knew she was going to a mass. I swear it, your Highness. I was so scared when I found out. But what could I do, stuck in a church in the middle of nowhere? I promise, I didn't join in, not once. I'm no Catholic. My family converted to the new religion as soon as we were told to."

She sounded so sincere and earnest, Jane felt sorry for her.

"Maud, why were you travelling with this woman?" asked Katherine.

"My parents have seven children to feed. It's too many, your Highness, so Father paid her a penny to bring me to London and find work. She was walking me to the city when someone on the road told us your house was looking for a girl for the kitchen. Mother always says, 'If you work close to food you'll never starve,' so I thought I should give it a try."

Katherine smiled. "Your mother sounds very wise. How old are you, Maud?"

"Only twelve, your Highness, but I'm strong. I worked on Lord Ware's estate where my father's one of the under-gardeners. I could do anything in your kitchen, your Highness, and I promise I'd work hard."

"I'm sure you would," said the queen but she looked doubtful.

"Please, your Highness," said the girl, dropping to her knees and clasping her hands beseechingly. "I can't go home. My mum can't manage all of us and there's another baby on the way. And with that woman arrested, I don't know the way to London or what to do when I get there."

Suddenly Jane had an idea. Maud seemed so nice and there was a position at Dormer Palace that was certainly vacant.

"Katherine," she said excitedly, "couldn't Maud look after me?"

The dowager queen smiled.

"What a good idea." She turned back to the girl. "Don't worry, Maud. This is Lady Jane Grey. I've been looking for a maid for her for some time and though you're young, I think you'll do nicely. Now come along and I'll have my secretary send a message to your family telling them you're safe and well. Did you say they live on Lord Ware's estate? Is that the one in Devon?"

"Yes, your Highness."

"Good. Then that's settled."

Jane was delighted. Somehow she knew Maud would be fun to have around.

Maud burst into Jane and Elizabeth's classroom. "Miss, miss! The Lord Admiral has a present for you!"

"Maud, I've asked you before, please knock," said Mr Aylmer, "and if it can wait until the afternoon, then let it."

"I'm sorry, sir, but I don't think it can."

"What is it?" asked Princess Elizabeth, disdainfully looking up from her work.

"Your Highness, it's the most beautiful dress you've ever seen. It must have cost the master a fortune."

The princess frowned and Mr Aylmer rolled his eyes. "We are studying the Greek philosophers. A dress can't possibly compare."

"This one might," said Maud boldly.

Jane smiled. Nine months had passed since Maud joined the household and she'd found her to be kind and loyal. She knew there was nothing her maid wouldn't do for her, but Maud did get overexcited. Growing up in Devon, the most she could have dreamed of was a position in a kitchen or dairy but instead she was a lady's maid in a royal household and she was enjoying every minute of it. Whether she was polishing the furniture, dusting the carpets or plumping up the feather mattresses, she took pleasure in her chores, but the thing she loved most of all was caring for Jane's wardrobe. She spent hours brushing and folding the velvet, silk and satin dresses, and nothing delighted her more than a new treasure to look after.

"I suppose it *is* almost midday," said Mr Aylmer resignedly. "Jane, you may go."

Minutes later they were in Jane's chamber.

"Here it is, miss. Isn't it beautiful?"

On the far side of the room was a large oak bed and spread out on the counterpane was a purple velvet robe and underskirt. It was trimmed with ermine at the collar and cuffs, and its petticoat was embroidered with pearls.

"I've never seen anything so lovely," said Maud, stroking the garment reverently. "And it came with a message from the master. You're to wear it tonight, Miss."

Jane held the dress up against her. There was no doubt it was exquisite but it made her strangely apprehensive. It was too much.

"Do you know why he bought it?" she asked.

Maud was excellent at picking up gossip. Late at night the maids, cooks and grooms gathered around the kitchen fire for a cup of beer and often the Lord Admiral's secretaries joined them. Alcohol loosened their tongues and Maud, sitting quietly in the corner, overheard many indiscretions. The Duke of Somerset had discovered Sir Thomas slipping money to the king and was furious, convinced his brother was trying to turn Edward against him; Princess Mary insisted on holding Catholic masses in her household despite the ban; and the Dorsets' debts were mounting again after a run of bad luck at cards.

But it seemed Maud had heard nothing about a dress. "No, miss. Could it be his way of celebrating the baby?"

A few months ago, Katherine had announced that she was pregnant.

"Surely he'd give something to his wife, not me," answered Jane.

"Then maybe he's thanking you for finding those Catholics."

"That was a long time ago. It must be something recent."

"Why is it bothering you, miss?" asked Maud.

"Because he's spent so much money. There has to be a reason. See if you can find out what it is."

The afternoon dragged by. As usual Elizabeth had disappeared, Katherine was resting and it was too wet to go outdoors. Jane was relieved when at last the clock struck seven and it was time for supper.

The oak-panelled dining room was on the far side of the house. As soon as Jane entered, Sir Thomas called, "Turn around. Let me have a look at you."

He was seated next to Elizabeth and opposite the dowager queen. Between them were several flickering candles, a large pie and a plate of roast partridge.

Feeling rather self-conscious in her new finery, Jane did as she was told.

"Come here, into the light," ordered the Lord Admiral, pulling over a silver candlestick. "What do you think, Elizabeth? Doesn't Jane look fine?"

"If you say so," answered the princess without looking up.

Sir Thomas nudged her with his elbow. "That's not much of an answer."

"Thomas, don't tease," remonstrated Katherine. "You're embarrassing Jane."

"I suppose you're right," said Sir Thomas genially and then he turned to the princess. "Elizabeth, you seem a little out of humour. Is there anything wrong? Would a visit to your brother help? We could all go to Greenwich Palace for Easter. Katherine, do you feel able to make the journey?"

"Never mind me, would Somerset allow it? Isn't he still fuming over the money you gave Edward?"

The Lord Admiral slammed his glass on the oak table so heavily it made Jane jump.

"Damn Somerset! The king is my nephew too! He's no right to keep the boy to himself."

"Calm down," said Katherine soothingly. "I'm sure we can visit his Majesty soon, but not at Greenwich Palace. There's plague south of London. Somerset has taken Edward to Richmond to keep him safe."

"Then we'll go there instead. Write and ask. No one can ever be angry with you. You can persuade him, I'm sure."

"I'll see what I can do," Katherine smiled. "Jane, sit down. Let's eat before the food gets cold."

It was almost ten o'clock by the time supper was over and Jane retired to her room, and as soon as she opened the door she could tell Maud had news.

"What is it?" she asked. "What have you found out?"

"To be honest, I don't understand it, miss," answered her maid, frowning. "I overheard one of the secretaries saying your parents have *sold* you, but that can't be right, can it?"

Jane sank down on the bed. For a moment she was too upset to answer. Sold her! Were her parents really so desperate they couldn't wait for the money her marriage would bring? And if they were, couldn't they at least have told her themselves?

"Can it possibly be true, miss?" asked Maud gently.

"Yes."

"Why?"

"I'm valuable and they're in debt."

"How are you valuable, miss?"

"If my parents sell me they get money to pay off their debts, and whoever buys me will get my marriage settlement. If that person can arrange a wealthy husband, they'll be rich. I'm in their hands now... I just wish I knew who they were."

"If the secretaries are right, miss, it's the Lord Admiral."

The Lord Admiral! thought Jane. This was unexpected,

but at least it solved the mystery of the dress. Sir Thomas was planning to start showing her off to possible suitors. But she liked her life at Dormer Palace and didn't want to be married off. Moreover the Lord Admiral was worryingly ambitious. Night after night he concocted one scheme after another: plans for usurping his brother, getting close to the king and securing a duchy. So what might he have in store for her? *But there's always Katherine!* thought Jane suddenly. *He never does anything without consulting her.* So perhaps this news wasn't so bad after all, for surely the kindly dowager queen would insist Jane ended up in a good home ... as long as Sir Thomas hadn't paid too much for her. If the Lord Admiral had borrowed money, even Katherine wouldn't be able to influence him. He would have to do his best to repay the debt.

"The secretaries didn't say how much he paid for me, did they?" asked Jane uneasily.

"They did, miss, and I couldn't believe the amount." Maud's eyes were wide with astonishment. "It was two thousand pounds – two hundred now and the rest to follow."

Two thousand pounds! Jane was astounded. How could she be worth two thousand pounds? It was enough money to buy Dormer Palace *and* Bradgate Hall. Her mind raced. Even in his wildest dreams, how could Sir Thomas possibly hope to sell her for more than that? Only a king could afford to pay that amount of money. Her heart sank. A marriage to Edward must be Sir Thomas's plan, but Jane didn't want to share her cousin's throne. She didn't want to be queen. Yet now, how could she avoid it?

14

"**Maud**, fetch Mrs Tack."

Katherine was sitting in a window seat, embroidering with Jane.

"I can't find her, your Highness," said the maid a few minutes later. "None of the servants has seen her since breakfast."

"This is ridiculous. There's so much to be done!"

A messenger had arrived that morning with a letter from Richmond Palace. Somerset had agreed that the Seymours could visit the king and now the housekeeper, Mrs Tack, must organize the packing.

"I'll see to it then," said Katherine, but as soon as she stood up the colour drained from her cheeks.

"Are you all right?" asked Jane.

"No. I feel dizzy again."

Katherine slumped into a chair, her head lolling alarmingly to one side.

"Katherine, can you hear me?" Jane whispered, heart pounding.

There was no response. Gently, she shook the dowager queen's shoulder.

"She's fainted, miss," said Maud. "My mum often did

that when she was expecting. If I loosen her ties and fan her, she should come around all right."

But Jane was in too much of a panic to listen.

"You stay with her. I'm going to ask the Lord Admiral to send for a doctor," she said, dashing from the room.

She hurried to Sir Thomas's study but he wasn't there. Quickly she checked the great hall and his parlour but both were empty.

In the long gallery one of the maids was polishing silver.

"Kitty, have you seen Sir Thomas?" she asked.

"I saw him in the garden, but that was a while ago, miss. Have you tried the Princess Elizabeth's apartments?"

"Why would he be there?"

The maid blushed. "It's just a thought, miss."

The princess's apartments were on the top floor of Dormer Palace, overlooking the ornamental gardens. Jane ran up the oak staircase two steps at a time. In front of her was a long corridor with a red-and-blue knotted carpet and walls hung with tapestries.

Maud had once told Jane that Elizabeth's apartments were the last rooms on the left... Or was it on the right? *No, I'm certain she said left*, thought Jane as she made her way along the passageway. The only sound was the creaking of floorboards. Now she was outside the door. She was about to knock when she heard a man's voice.

"Elizabeth, you can't *still* be angry."

It was Sir Thomas.

"I'm not angry. You may do as you please."

"Then why are you making such a fuss? It was only a dress," sighed the Lord Admiral. "You know I'd buy you a dozen dresses, if you wanted me to."

His familiar tone made Jane uneasy. Surely Elizabeth would protest. Instead Jane heard a giggle that made her stomach turn. Something was going on between them – but Elizabeth was only fourteen and Sir Thomas was married with a pregnant wife downstairs! Jane had an overwhelming desire to get away. She turned and ran straight into Mrs Ashley, Elizabeth's governess.

"Can I help you, miss?"

Mrs Ashley was a prim young woman in a grey dress buttoned up to her neck.

Jane blushed, ashamed to be caught eavesdropping.

"I was looking for the princess," she mumbled.

"Then knock, miss."

But just then the door opened and there was the Lord Admiral, and behind him Elizabeth, flushed and adjusting the shoulders of her bodice.

"Ah Mrs Ashley. I came to tell the princess that we're expected at Richmond Palace," said Sir Thomas breezily.

It was quite improper for him to be alone in an unmarried girl's apartment, let alone a princess's, but he showed not the slightest sign of embarrassment.

"Jane, what are you doing here?" he asked.

"Katherine's unwell," she said, unable to look him in the eye. "She needs a doctor."

"Then we must go to her immediately. Come along."

Jane followed him reluctantly. *How could he be so callous? And how could Elizabeth treat her stepmother so cruelly?* She felt sick to her stomach. Dormer Palace was no longer the happy home she'd imagined it to be.

15

The poppies were in full bloom but Jane was in too much of a hurry to enjoy them. That morning, before breakfast, she'd left a note in Katherine's parlour asking her to come down to the river at midday. She hadn't signed it because she had wanted to surprise her with a picnic. But infuriatingly, Mr Aylmer had insisted she stay behind to finish an Italian translation and now she was going to be late. Katherine would be wondering what was going on.

By the time Jane had collected the basket of food from Mrs Tack and run to the riverbank she was over half an hour late and there was no sign of the dowager queen. She stamped her foot crossly. She'd so wanted to surprise Katherine! Then Jane thought of the rose garden next to the river. Perhaps Katherine was waiting there.

The picnic hamper was heavy with ox tongue pie, prune cake and a bottle of beer, but Jane heaved it across the lawn, past a tall willow tree, and through an arch cut into a hawthorn hedge. Ahead was a sunny, secluded spot, with two stone benches and beds of lush red roses and drooping lavender. Unfortunately there was no sign of Katherine.

She must have gone back to the house, thought Jane.

I must go and apologize. It's so annoying; I was only trying to cheer her up.

Ever since her fainting fit, Katherine had been so listless she'd hardly left the palace. The doctor had advised that with a pregnancy at her age it wasn't safe to travel and so she'd even missed the trip to Richmond Palace. *And a good thing too*, thought Jane. Those seven days at court had been humiliating. Sir Thomas had paraded her around in that purple gown from dawn until dusk telling anyone who would listen that she was a new religionist, a Tudor and a perfect match for the king! But to Jane's relief, Somerset was firmly against the idea and Sir Thomas was forced to retreat back to Chelsea.

She stopped for a moment and put down the hamper to catch her breath. She couldn't stop thinking about the dowager queen. *It would be all right if tiredness were her only problem*, she thought, *but there's the wretched business of Sir Thomas and Elizabeth.*

"It seems everybody in the household knew but us, miss," Maud had whispered late one night. "They're often in the garden together *and* he visits her bedroom early in the morning before she's dressed. He's even had a copy made of the key to her apartments."

"Are you sure Katherine doesn't know?" Jane had asked.

"I'm certain. And Mrs Tack says woe betide the person that tells her, in her delicate state."

Jane could hardly believe Sir Thomas would behave so badly to his wife and was even more horrified when Maud discovered the probable reason for his affair. If Katherine died in childbirth, his secretaries whispered, he planned to marry Elizabeth. Mary was too old for children and Edward was sickly. It might not be too long before the princess inherited the throne.

Jane picked up the hamper again and climbed the steps of the stone terrace to the parlour door. She was just about to knock when a furious scream stopped her. It was Katherine! Jane had never even heard her raise her voice before.

She paused, unsure what to do next, when the dowager queen cried out, "Thomas, how could you? The girl's half your age and she's my stepdaughter."

She knows! thought Jane. Part of her was relieved. For the past month, she'd squirmed each time Elizabeth sent her governess on errands in Chelsea so Sir Thomas could steal up the back stairs.

"You're imagining it," she heard Sir Thomas protest. "And anyway there are more pressing things to worry about."

"Not for me, there aren't. Someone left me a note telling me to go to the river and I saw you there, kissing in the rose garden. People must be laughing at the mistress who can't see what's happening under her very nose."

Jane had heard enough. She crept away sadly, carrying her hamper. *What a terrible coincidence!* she thought. *It was my note that brought poor Katherine there…*

She didn't know what to do. Should she admit she

had left the letter or would that just make things worse? And if she didn't own up, she might even get away with it. After all, nobody had seen her leave the note and she hadn't told Mrs Tack who the picnic was for. What was best?

Quickly she retraced her steps to the river. She needed a place to think. She passed through the arch to the rose garden and sat down on the nearest stone bench, but a moment later she heard footsteps. It was Elizabeth. Her heart started racing.

The princess's dark eyes burned angrily as she marched over and tossed a piece of paper onto Jane's lap.

"Your handwriting, I believe," she spat. "It's thanks to you I'm being sent away. I suppose that's what you wanted."

Without another word, she turned and stormed off.

Jane chased after her.

"Your Highness, I never meant this to happen! I didn't know you and the Lord Admiral would be meeting here, I swear."

Elizabeth turned around, her hands on her hips and face white with fury.

"I don't believe you! Ever since you found him in my room, I knew you'd do something like this. Don't you think things are bad enough for me already?"

"What do you mean?" Jane was confused.

"My mother was beheaded for treason. Everywhere I go, people whisper about her – and me. And now,

because of you, they'll have even more to gossip about."
The princess was shaking. "But remember this. One way
or another, I'll get my revenge... I'll never forget what
you've done to me."

And as Jane watched Elizabeth walk away, she was
certain she meant every word she said.

Jane sank back down on the stone bench, trembling all over. Elizabeth hated her and presumably, once the princess had told him who had sent the note, Sir Thomas would too. Then how long would it be before she was banished back to Bradgate Hall?

A bumble bee buzzed around her head and after a while she flicked it away and got to her feet. She couldn't hide in the rose garden any longer. She had to find out what was in store for her.

She was only halfway across the lawn when she saw Sir Thomas. As he hurried down the steps towards her, she braced herself for the onslaught, but instead he said, "Jane! Thank God I've found you."

"What is it?" she asked, surprised.

"Plague. A case has been discovered in Chelsea. We must leave straight away."

For a moment, Jane's legs turned to jelly. Chelsea was less than a mile away and the dangerous vapours might already be among them. Three years ago there had been an outbreak of plague in Leicestershire and Jane had never forgotten Mistress Ellen's ghoulish description of its first victim. "A blacksmith went to bed early feeling unwell, and by midnight he was covered in hideous lumps. By morning he was dead. His wife swore she'd never seen anything like it. She said it was the devil's work, his ending was so terrible."

More and more cases had been discovered. The deadly disease was carried on the wind and no curtains or shutters were strong enough to keep it out. Infected houses chalked "Lord, have mercy upon us" on their doors but it made no difference. The plague kept spreading until one day a stable boy at Bradgate Hall had fallen ill. That afternoon the Dorsets fled and when they finally returned, over half the servants had died. And now it was here, at the gates of Dormer Palace.

"What about Katherine?" Jane asked. "Is it safe to move her?"

"It'll have to be," said Sir Thomas grimly. "Fortunately, Elizabeth was already leaving." He blushed. "She has been unexpectedly called away to Cheshunt. Now we must leave too. So hurry! Get your things! There's not a moment to lose."

"Miss! It's started! said Maud excitedly as she opened Jane's shutters two days later.

Jane sat up, rubbing her eyes.

"What do you mean?"

"The baby – it's coming!"

Suddenly Jane was wide awake. Katherine was exhausted by their hurried dash from Chelsea. They'd arrived at Sudeley Manor only a few days ago and since then she'd spent all her time resting in a darkened room. Each evening when Jane visited, she was appalled by how frail the dowager queen was. She hardly ate and would not see Sir Thomas. Could she really be strong enough to give birth?

Jane spent all morning pacing the gardens, desperately hoping that Katherine and the baby would both be all right... That the labour wasn't too hard... That nothing would go wrong.

At midday, Maud came running to find her.

"It's over, miss," she shouted happily, "and the dowager queen wants to see you."

Jane rushed back to the house. Katherine was propped up in bed, her cheeks as pale as her nightgown, and in her arms was a tiny swaddled bundle.

"Is it a boy or a girl?" asked Jane, tiptoeing forwards.

"Sir Thomas will be disappointed. It's a girl. Say hello to little Mary."

Jane studied the pink crinkled face, the wisps of hair and the delicate fingers.

"She's beautiful," she said. "I'm so glad you're both safe."

But Jane had spoken too soon. The next evening the dowager queen developed a fever. By morning the fever had turned to delirium and within a week Katherine was dead.

17

"**What's** that banging?"

Jane sat up. Her night candle had burnt out and the chamber was pitch-black. Had she imagined the noise in her sleep? No – there it was again. *Knock, knock, knock!* Someone was hammering on the front door.

Shivering in her linen nightgown, she climbed out of bed and opened a shutter, letting in a shaft of moonlight. Now she could see the trundle cot where Maud was sleeping. She shook her maid.

"Maud, someone's at the door! Wake up."

"What's going on, miss?"

Maud was bleary eyed, her curly hair tangled.

"I don't know, but it must be to do with the Lord Admiral."

Jane had been dreading something like this. Six months ago, after Katherine's funeral, her parents had recalled her to Bradgate Hall, saying they would find a husband for their daughter themselves. They'd lost confidence in Sir Thomas, who owed them money. To make matters worse, Somerset was rumoured to be negotiating for Mary, Queen of Scots, to marry King Edward. But Jane had not been home long before Sir

Thomas came to report that, far from the Scottish queen heading to London, she'd been spirited away to France, England's enemy. Somerset was humiliated and the time was right for Jane. Sir Thomas had managed to raise five hundred pounds and easily persuaded the Dorsets to return Jane to him, so, last October, she had travelled south to his London residence.

Jane had now spent four months at Seymour Place, a beautiful mansion just inside the city walls, with a large garden running down to the river. But she was not happy. She missed Katherine and, without the good sense of his wife, Sir Thomas's schemes were getting out of hand.

"They're inside," whispered Maud, her green eyes wide with fear, as they heard the front door open.

"Everyone downstairs!" shouted an angry voice.

Jane's hands were shaking. *Calm down!* she told herself. It was probably nothing to do with her.

The flag-stoned hall was packed with soldiers, and the household's servants, still in their nightshirts and caps, were crowded together like a flock of frightened sheep.

"Lady Jane Grey," said an elderly soldier with a shock of white hair, stubble on his chin and an enormous lump the size of an egg protruding from his neck. "I am Sir John Brydges, Lieutenant of the Tower of London. Tell me, where is the coward hiding?"

"What do you mean, Sir John?" Jane asked, trying to stop her voice from quivering.

"The Lord Admiral – where is he?"

"I don't know. I haven't seen him since supper," Jane answered truthfully.

Suddenly there was a furious cry from the gallery.

"I've found him!" shouted a soldier, dragging Sir Thomas downstairs.

Jane was shocked. She'd only ever seen her guardian in the latest fashions – silk doublets, ostrich feathers, velvet capes and leather jerkins – but now his hose was around his ankles, his shirt was unbuttoned and he looked terrified.

"I've done nothing wrong!" he yelled, his eyes swivelling like a madman. "Brydges, I swear my brother will kill you for this."

"I doubt it," smirked the officer. "He ordered your arrest."

The soldiers sniggered impertinently and a moment later Sir Thomas was bundled through the front door in an undignified scuffle.

"Where are you taking him?" Jane asked the last guard.

"To the Tower, miss, where he belongs. Now all of you, get back to bed."

"That's the one place I'm not going," said a footman once the door was shut. "The master won't be coming back but that lot will. They'll want to know who's been visiting Sir Thomas and they won't be asking nicely."

"He's right," said a scullery boy. "If we're not careful

we'll end up in the Tower with him. I'm leaving while I still can."

"But what about the curfew?" moaned a dumpy washerwoman. "I don't want to be mistaken for a robber."

"I'd rather risk that than be caught in a traitor's house."

And suddenly the servants were scurrying this way and that, packing bundles of clothes and blankets before disappearing into the night.

"What should we do, miss?" asked Maud when they were left alone.

"I suppose we should wait until someone comes for us," Jane said doubtfully.

"I don't like being here all alone," said Maud.

"Neither do I," admitted Jane. "Let's go upstairs."

But the bedchamber was just as unsettling. Jane tried to sleep, but her mind was whirring. What did Sir Thomas's arrest mean? Would she be returned to her hated home? Or sold to another guardian? She tossed and turned restlessly. Then suddenly she heard the tinkle of glass.

"Someone's breaking in," whispered Maud.

There was the sound of a crash.

"We're being robbed, miss! And we're all alone. They might kill us!"

Suddenly Jane knew she couldn't spend another moment in this creepy house.

"Maud, we're leaving," she said.

"What about the curfew? It takes so long to dress you."

They heard heavy footsteps downstairs.

"You can lend me some of your clothes."

Swiftly they pulled on Maud's two scratchy brown wool dresses, a shawl each and a white cap. Maud put on her clogs and Jane her leather walking boots.

"Wait. I must take Katherine's necklace," she said, remembering her most treasured possession – the gold chain and cross she'd been left in the dowager queen's will.

Maud dug around in the chest. "It's here."

They tiptoed to the door. Jane opened it an inch and saw the light of a flaming torch moving around the hall below. Someone was searching the downstairs rooms.

"Come on," she beckoned to Maud.

They crept along the gallery to the servants' spiral staircase and flew down the steps. Moments later, they slipped safely out of the back door into a narrow street, far from Seymour Place's grand river entrance.

"Where do we go now, miss?" asked Maud.

Jane bit her lip. She hadn't thought beyond getting out of the house.

"I don't know," she answered.

"There must be someone in the city," pressed Maud.

Jane was about to shake her head when suddenly she remembered Ferdinand. He would surely be at the Carpenters' Guild. She hadn't seen him for over a year and a half, since he'd accompanied her on the long ride to Dormer Palace, but she knew he would help her if he could.

She hugged Maud.

"There might just be someone. Come on."

18

"**Remember**, we mustn't make a sound."

It was a frosty January night. Jane pulled her woollen shawl close, but she was still cold and her toes were numb.

"Which way?" mouthed Maud.

Despite spending months in London, Jane barely knew the city. She'd spent most of her time at Seymour Place and on the rare occasions when Sir Thomas paraded her at court, she was collected by a fancy wherry at the elegant landing stage at the bottom of the garden and rowed to Richmond, Greenwich or Whitehall Palace.

The city was as mysterious and unknown to her as the first day she'd arrived – a warren of narrow, dirty streets filled with traders and beggars. But she remembered the grand Carpenters' Guild on Cheapside – a wide street close to St Paul's Cathedral. *The cathedral! Of course! That was the direction they must go in.*

"That way!" she said, pointing at its towering spire. "Come on."

In the deserted streets every shutter was closed, but there was always the chance of a nightwatchman seeing them on his rounds. They had to be careful.

Staying in the shadows, they made good progress

towards the vast spire that dominated the skyline. At every corner they stopped to check there was no one about. Once they heard snorts and snuffles but it was only pigs rummaging in a pile of rubbish. Another time a window opened above them and the foul contents of a chamber pot came splashing down, missing them by inches.

By the time the city bells tolled half past five they'd reached the front steps of the cathedral. *Not long to go now*, thought Jane happily, for once the sun was up the night-watchmen's duties would end, the streets would fill and they could disappear into the crowds.

They climbed the great stone steps of the cathedral, searching for Cheapside. *I know it's around here somewhere*, Jane thought. Then she turned and saw a broad street paved with flint-stones.

"Down there!" she whispered to Maud. "Stay close to the buildings – we're easy to spot."

They ran across the street and hurried eastward past the grand Mercers' Hall. They couldn't be far from the Carpenters' Guild.

"There it is!" said Jane, pointing jubilantly to a large building with a painted coat of arms on the front. "We'll find somewhere to hide until the curfew is over and then I'll knock on the door."

But just then someone grabbed her shoulder. They'd been caught.

19

"**What** are you doing here?" said a rough voice.

Jane turned around. She was being held by an elderly nightwatchman dressed in a battered leather jerkin and a black, brimmed hat. His face was weathered, he had a straggly beard and not a single tooth, but despite his age his grip on her shoulder was surprisingly strong.

"I said, what are you doing here? You know you're not allowed on the streets at this time. I'll have to take you to the sheriff."

Maud turned white. "Oh please, sir! Don't do that," she begged.

"Yes, please let us go," said Jane. Not only would they be punished for being out on the streets during the curfew but she might be found out and accused of plotting with Sir Thomas. She should have stayed at Seymour Place and hidden from that wretched robber.

"I can't," said the nightwatchman. "It's what I'm paid for and you two will earn me a pretty couple of pennies. Now what are your names and where are you going?"

Jane and Maud stared at him blankly. And just then church bells began to chime. It was six o'clock. The curfew was over. If only he had spotted them a couple of minutes later everything would have been all right.

"Sir, it's six in the morning," she pleaded. "We were only a few minutes early. It was a mistake – honestly."

"No doubt it was. But the law's the law. Now – names?"

With the sound of the bells, the street began to fill surprisingly quickly. Servants brought out chamber pots to empty in the gutter and hurried to fill jugs from the fountains in the centre of the street, while the tradesmen began setting up their stalls for the day.

Jane racked her mind for something – anything – that might persuade the man to let them go. "We only wanted to see our ... brother," she said, thinking of Ferdinand. "He's an apprentice at the Carpenters' Guild. If we don't catch him early we never see him as our mistress keeps us busy from dawn till dusk."

Just then a plump woman with a honking goose under each arm pushed past.

"We're getting in everyone's way," said the night-watchman wearily. "You can explain all this to the sheriff."

He propelled them along the crowded pavement, a hand on each of their shoulders. *This is all my fault*, thought Jane miserably, *and now Maud's in trouble too.*

"Oi! Watch out."

Jane turned round. The nightwatchman was shouting at a dark-haired boy with a bowl of slopping water.

"Look what you've done! I'm soaked."

"I'm sorry," apologized the boy, and then he gasped. "Jane? Is that you?"

It was Ferdinand! He was several inches taller, and leaner around the face, but the olive skin and brown eyes were unmistakeable.

"So this is your brother, is it?" asked the nightwatchman, shaking his wet sleeve.

"Yes," said Jane quickly, silently begging Ferdinand not to say a word.

"He doesn't look much like you."

"We share a mother, not a father," she said hastily. "Please let us talk to him and then we'll be on our way."

To her relief the old man shrugged. "Well I suppose there's no harm in it. But make sure I don't catch you again. I won't be so soft-hearted next time."

"What's going on?" asked Ferdinand as soon as the man was out of earshot.

Briefly, Jane told him what had happened.

"News of Sir Thomas's arrest whistled round the guild this morning," said Ferdinand, "but I had no idea you were staying with him. I suppose you want to get home now?"

"To Bradgate Hall?" Jane shook her head. "I never want to go there again." Suddenly she knew what she wanted. "I want to disappear... I'll become a maid with Maud, or one of those flower sellers. Anything but go back to my old life."

Ferdinand took her hand.

"You can't just abandon your family, Jane."

"Why not? They don't care about me."

"They must, in their own way. And Jane, you don't

know what work is. You don't know what it is like – having no money, always wondering where your next meal is coming from. It's not the life for you."

"I could try..." Jane said weakly.

"No. You'll be safer at home. Wait here and I'll see what I can do."

Jane and Maud sat down on the stone steps of the Carpenters' Guild, rubbing their chilly hands as they watched the busy street in silence. It felt like forever before Ferdinand returned with a knapsack and a couple of blankets.

"We're going to have to rough it. I've only a few pennies but that'll be enough, if we're careful."

"What do you mean, 'if we're careful'?" asked Jane. "Surely you can't leave your apprenticeship."

"Yes I can," said Ferdinand triumphantly. "I told the master I've had some bad news and need to go home. He agreed to give me two weeks off as long as I work the next three months of Sundays. Now, come on!"

For four days Jane, Ferdinand and Maud journeyed north along the main road from London. To begin with, luck was with them. As they passed through Lud Gate, Ferdinand noticed an empty wagon pulled by two enormous grey shire horses. Sitting in the front were a farmer and his wife returning home from market. The couple were not in the least bit curious about three children travelling alone. They'd often seen sons or daughters of families too poor to keep them looking for work and got straight down to haggling over the fare. For half a penny and the toll charge they said they'd take them as far as their farm near Hatfield.

All day the wagon lumbered on, reaching the farm at dusk. The children camped in the barn and were given a bowl of soup and some goat's cheese for supper.

The next morning they'd walked less than a mile before Ferdinand negotiated an even longer ride, this time on a cart taking silks to Peterborough. The driver was glad of their company. The cloth was expensive and there were often bandits on the road so that night they took turns guarding the precious load while the carter rigged up a tent, downed a bottle of beer and fell asleep by the fire.

For the next two days they plodded on. Gradually villages and farms changed from the grey stone of the south to the red brick of the Midlands.

By the afternoon of the fourth day, they reached a bleak crossroads surrounded by turnip fields.

"This is where we separate," announced the driver. "I go east and you west towards Dimsford. But hurry. The weather's not looking too good and there's nothing between here and there."

"How far is it?" asked Ferdinand.

"A good three miles, I reckon. There's one of those old shrines at the top of the valley and the village is below it."

"How much further is Leicester?" asked Jane.

"Less than fifteen miles. With luck you'll be there by tomorrow's sunset."

As the cart disappeared around a corner in the winding track the wind picked up and snowflakes began drifting down from the leaden sky.

"I'm freezing," said Maud, pulling her shawl tightly around her.

"So am I," said Ferdinand, "and there won't be any wagons out in this weather."

"Well it's too cold to stay here," said Jane. "We'd better get walking."

They trudged along the muddy road between two tall hedgerows. The wind whipped through their woollen clothes and soon snow was falling fast. It wasn't long before they were soaked and to make matters worse,

Maud's clogs began to rub. She struggled along for a while and then stopped, tore a strip of linen from her apron and wrapped it around her feet.

"At this rate we'll never reach Dimsford by dark," said Ferdinand after a painfully slow half mile.

"Then we'll just have to keep going until we do," answered Jane.

But the drifting snow made each step exhausting and Maud was lagging further and further behind.

"Are you all right?" called Jane.

Maud shook her head.

"I can't go on."

She sank to the ground and, despite the snow, kicked off her clogs. Her bandaged toes were covered in blood. Jane was horrified. Maud must be in great pain, but it was freezing and almost dark. They couldn't rest for long.

"What if we shelter on the other side of the hedge for a minute?" she asked desperately.

Maud hobbled the few yards to a gate.

"Climb over," said Jane encouragingly, though she knew the gnarled hedge would provide little protection from the biting wind. And then something caught her eye.

"Wait," she said, peering over the gate. "There's a light."

"That's impossible," said Ferdinand. "You heard the carter. There's nothing for miles around."

"Then someone's set up a camp."

"Not in this weather. You're imagining it."

"I'm not. Look."

Ferdinand climbed the wooden gate, stared into the distance, and grudgingly admitted there might be something there.

"Let's find out what it is," said Jane.

"I don't think we should," he said. "At least if we stick to the road we'll hear if a cart passes."

"But you said yourself, there'll be nobody about in this weather."

Jane helped Maud over the gate and they began walking towards the flickering light. By the time Ferdinand caught them up they were halfway across the rutted field.

"Come back," he pleaded.

"No," said Jane. "Look!"

Miraculously, a large grey building with arched windows, turrets and a tower emerged from the flurries of snow.

"It must be an abandoned monastery," said Jane. "Maybe someone's sheltering there and will let us sit by their fire. It's better than freezing out here."

21

"**We** shouldn't go in," said Ferdinand.

They were standing beside two large wooden doors, one hanging off its hinges – the entrance to the ruined abbey.

"We can't stay out here," said Jane, stamping her numb feet.

Awkwardly she scrambled over the broken door and found herself in a pitch-black room. She waited a moment, while her eyes adjusted to the dark and made out a stone staircase and there, at the top, the flickering light she had seen from the road.

"Come on," she whispered, not wanting to be alone in the eerie building.

Ferdinand came next, followed by Maud.

"I don't like it here," said Maud, taking hold of Jane's arm. "It's too dark."

"Then let's go upstairs to the light."

"But we don't know who's up there," protested Ferdinand. "It's not safe."

"What choice do we have?" asked Jane exasperatedly. The hall was as damp and cold as the field outside. "It's probably some other frozen travellers."

The steps were worn, with several loose stones. Cautiously, she led the way up and then jumped as a pale young man with a bent nose and sallow skin stepped out from the shadows. He looked strangely familiar.

"Who's there?" he called.

Suddenly Ferdinand was by her side, pulling a string of wooden beads from his pocket.

"Wait – I know you," he said. "You're John Hawker! My name is Ferdinand Mallet and I'm one of you. We saw the light and came to take shelter from the blizzard. I'm surprised to see you here."

John Hawker! – I know that name, thought Jane. Where had she heard it before? Suddenly she remembered – the hidden church in the forest! It was the name of the peddler Sir Thomas had arrested. She stared at him. Same beaky nose and hooded grey eyes... And then she noticed a single pink ribbon peeking out from the pocket of his battered coat. It *was* him. But how on earth did he and Ferdinand know each other?

"Ferdinand Mallet," Hawker was saying. "Of course – Richard and Isabella's son." He smiled at Maud. "And you're the girl we hid under the altar in that chapel in Chelsea. You managed to get away!" He turned to Jane, his eyes narrowing. "And who are you?"

"She's my sister," Ferdinand answered quickly.

"I thought Isabella's daughters all died." The peddler looked confused.

"All but one. Jane was away when the plague struck."

As they spoke, Jane stared at the wooden rosary dangling from Ferdinand's hand – a chain of beads threaded on red silk with knots separating them into little groups of ten and a small wooden cross hanging from the middle. It came to her that though he was her friend they had never once talked about faith or religion. Now she understood why.

Just then a bell tinkled.

"The service is about to begin," said the peddler. "Go in – true believers are always welcome."

Before she had time to protest Ferdinand grabbed her arm.

"You insisted we come," he said grimly, "and now we're here. Stay in the shadows and say nothing. I can't protect you if you're discovered."

Jane awoke with a jolt. She'd planned to lie under her blanket until everyone was asleep and then slip away but two of the wretched Catholics had sat up by the fire talking late into the night and somehow she must have drifted off. She glanced out of the window. The sky was barely grey so she could only have been sleeping for an hour at most but she was still furious with herself. She must leave soon and definitely before daybreak. She couldn't risk being recognized by the peddler in the brighter morning light.

Cautiously she looked about her. She was surrounded by sleeping figures, any of whom could stir at any moment. She rose quietly and searched for her boots, finding them next to the fireplace. As she pulled them on someone caught at her dress. It was Maud.

"Where are you going?" the maid whispered groggily, pushing her hair from her eyes.

"I'm leaving," hissed Jane.

"Why?"

"Because you're all filthy Catholics!"

She was halfway down the stairs before Maud came scurrying after her.

"You can't think that!" she pleaded.

"Why not?" said Jane angrily. "Do you think I'm stupid? I found you in that chapel years ago and last night during the service you knew exactly what to do."

"That's only because I remembered it," said Maud. "Until a few years ago, we heard mass in our village every week. Then Lord Ware announced that we had to practice the new religion and we didn't want any trouble so we did as we were told. I suppose you could say I used to be a Catholic but you can't blame me for it. Everybody was then."

Maud looked so sincere Jane found it impossible not to believe her. "I'm sorry, Maud," she said. "Forgive me?"

"Of course," said Maud. "Shall I fetch Ferdinand?"

Jane shook her head

"No. He *is* Catholic."

"Only because his mother's Spanish. He explained it to me last night while you were sleeping. The old faith's sacred to her and she couldn't abandon it just because a foreign king told her to, but of course the family had to keep it secret or they'd have been sent to prison. He didn't dare tell a soul... Not even you."

"If he's Catholic, he's a traitor," said Jane stubbornly.

"Oh, Jane," said Maud. "Look what he's done for you. And besides, has he really done anything so wrong? He still believes in the Bible, he just worships in a different way – the way his mother taught him, just as you worship the way your parents taught you."

"You can't compare us," said Jane indignantly. "I'd have converted to the truth whatever family I was born into."

"Are you sure?" asked Maud.

"Of course I am. The truth is the truth."

"But King Henry was Catholic and so were your parents and the Seymours and everyone else before the old king's marriage to Anne Boleyn—"

"Stop it!" said Jane. "I won't hear another word. If Ferdinand is Catholic, I'll have nothing to do with him. Now, decide. Do you want to come with me or stay here with him?"

"I'll come with you," said Maud.

"Good. Then let's go and don't ever mention his name again."

Five years later
Spring 1553

"Miss Jane, your parents want you," said Mistress Ellen. "They're in the parlour."

Jane sighed, put her book on the table and went downstairs.

The parlour was grand but unwelcoming, its floor, ceiling and walls covered with gloomy oak panelling. She knocked at the open door wondering, *What is it now?*

Her parents were seated opposite each other in two high-backed chairs. Lord Dorset's cheeks were ruddy from sitting too close to the fire while Lady Dorset was still in her mud-spattered riding habit. Over the years she'd become heavier and she was now a formidable sight in yards of russet velvet.

"You sent for me?" asked Jane, curtseying.

Lady Dorset pulled off a glove and beckoned to her daughter.

"See what I mean, Henry?" she said. "We can't leave it much longer. I know she'll never be a beauty but her skin's not bad and ... Jane, open your mouth ... and, see, her teeth are white." She reached out and squeezed Jane's bosom, "And she's got a decent bust."

Instinctively Jane pushed her mother's hand away, earning herself a sharp slap on the wrist.

"So Henry, what do you think?"

Lord Dorset pursed his thick wet lips.

"How old are you, Jane?"

"Fifteen."

"And the business with Sir Thomas..."

"Oh that's long forgotten," said Lady Dorset dismissively. "It's five years since that fool was beheaded."

Had it really been five years since that midnight dash from Seymour Place? thought Jane. When she'd finally arrived home, her parents had been furious with her. But they'd grudgingly conceded that now that she was safely in Leicestershire it was prudent for her to lie low at Bradgate Hall until the whole ugly business of the Lord Admiral's arrest blew over. They'd even let her keep Maud as her maid.

In the months that followed her flight, wild tales spread from London. Elizabeth was interrogated and her affair with Sir Thomas soon became common knowledge – it was rumoured the princess only saved her life by swearing she would never have married without consulting the king. The Lord Admiral was less fortunate. Somerset, fuming over his brother's endless plotting, persuaded Edward to behead him for treason. But it wasn't long before Somerset suffered the same fate himself, and now the Duke of Northumberland was said to be the most powerful man in the land.

"What about the king?" asked Lord Dorset, turning to his wife. "I've heard he's coughing up black phlegm and the doctors haven't got a clue what to do. It might be wiser to stay away from court, until he's better."

For many months rumours had been swirling around about Edward's health. In the autumn he'd been well enough to conduct a three-month tour of the West Country but shortly after returning to Westminster he'd fallen ill with an ugly chest infection.

"Henry, he might not *get* better," snapped his wife. "Don't you see? We've kept Jane away from court for too long. We must go to London, or we'll miss out. Northumberland won't wait for us."

"What's it got to do with Northumberland?"

"He's the most powerful man in the land." Lady Dorset sounded exasperated. "If the king dies, what then? Mary is the next in line for the throne but she's Catholic so he won't want her. Perhaps it's a chance for Jane."

"But last time she was in London, it was a disaster."

"That's because we let her ruin it." Lady Dorset pointed accusingly at her daughter. "We won't make that mistake again. She'll only join us once her marriage is finalized."

And so, thought Jane sadly, her time far from the intrigues of court had finally come to an end, as she had always feared it would.

24

Jane stood in front of a polished steel mirror. Her face was powdered white, her cheeks and lips painted scarlet and her hair tucked under a violet headdress. She was wearing an elaborate lavender gown so encrusted with pearls that it cut into her shoulders.

She stared at the glass, hardly recognizing herself.

"Maud, remember not to pull on her train or she'll trip," ordered Lady Dorset.

"Yes, ma'am."

"Good. Then let's go."

Lady Dorset marched down the deserted corridor. Greenwich was the most sumptuous palace in the land, famed for extravagant banquets, dances and jousts. During King Henry's reign there had been masked balls that lasted until dawn, tournaments, musicians, hunts and elaborate plays. But not any more, for King Edward was desperately ill.

By the time Jane's barge docked at the grand jetty on the River Thames, the palace was hushed and desolate. The last days of a monarch were dangerous times and many courtiers fled to the safety of their country estates. Those that remained huddled in quiet corners and faraway turrets contemplating what might happen next. Would Catholic Mary really become queen? Or would Elizabeth, a bastard but a new-religionist, be better? And wouldn't any woman be a disaster? There was a reason England had never had a queen, for how could a woman possibly rule?

"Mother, are you sure this dress isn't too colourful, in the circumstances?" Jane asked apprehensively.

"Of course not. We're not in mourning yet."

They reached the Great Hall, where Lord Dorset was waiting for them.

"What took you so long?" he hissed. "We're late paying our respects."

"Henry, calm down. Jane has to look right."

Lord Dorset glanced at his daughter.

"That's all very well, Frances, but even you can't keep Northumberland waiting."

"If you're ready, my Lord," said a bored soldier in yellow and blue striped pantaloons. "I will escort you."

They left the cavernous hall behind and entered the king's private apartments.

The soldier led them along a grand passageway until at last they reached two doors painted in red and gold – the king's bedroom.

"Lord and Lady Dorset and their daughter, the Lady Jane Grey," announced the guard.

Nervously, Jane followed her parents into the gloomy chamber with Maud still clutching her train.

Before her was the most elaborate bed she'd ever seen, a

four poster stretching up almost to the ceiling with green damask curtains edged with gold fringe. Propped up on feather pillows was the king. Jane hardly recognized him. His face was hideously swollen and covered with ugly sores, and he was bald except for a few wispy ginger tufts. His eyes were closed and he struggled for breath.

To one side of the bed were three men. Two were worried-looking physicians, austerely dressed in black hats and robes. The third was a bulky man with a thick dark beard cut to a point over his stiff white collar. He wore a red jacket and hose under a sumptuous fur-lined coat. He could only be the Duke of Northumberland, Somerset's ambitious replacement.

Jane dropped a deep curtsey. As she rose Northumberland dismissed the doctors with a flick of his hand, leaned on the king's shoulder and whispered into his ear.

With an effort, Edward roused himself.

"Lady Jane, is that you?" His voice was hoarse.

"Yes, your Majesty," she murmured.

"Come closer."

Jane was appalled. He was a pitiful sight. But against every instinct, she took several steps until she was only inches from the bed. Now she could see his sheets were stained with pus, his face was waxy and he had crusts of spittle at the corners of his mouth. She glanced at his hands and saw that the tips of his fingers were black and only one nail remained.

"What is it, your Majesty?" she asked gently.

Again Northumberland leaned forward, planting words in the dying boy's mouth.

"Jane, are you a true believer?" asked the king with great effort.

"Of course, your Majesty."

"And are you in good health?"

"Yes, your Majesty. I am very well."

Edward turned to Northumberland. "Then let it be done," he said, before collapsing back onto his pillow.

Her engagement must have been approved, but Jane still had no idea who she would marry.

"**When** will they tell you, Miss?" asked Maud when at last she and Jane had a moment alone.

Jane sat wearily on a stool by a window overlooking the river. The tide was out, revealing grey muddy banks strewn with rubbish. It was grim – almost as grim as she felt.

"Soon enough."

"And who do you think it will be, miss?" asked Maud gently.

"One of the duke's cronies, I suppose, since he's arranged it."

"I know it's not my place, miss, but I didn't like the look of him," said Maud as she busied herself tidying the already immaculate room.

A moment later, the apartment door was pushed open without even the courtesy of a knock and in walked Lord and Lady Dorset with Northumberland and a young man Jane had never seen before. He was fair skinned with a clean-shaven boyish face and was fashionably dressed in white hose and short puffy trousers of silver silk with a matching cape.

He can only be a couple of years older than me, thought

Jane. *And he's very slight ... almost girlish.*

"Leave us, Maud," ordered her mother.

Once the maid had left, Lord Dorset cleared his throat.

"Jane, we have someone we'd like you to meet," he said. "As you know, your mother and I have thought long and hard about finding you a suitable husband and we think you'll agree we've found the perfect match."

Impatiently, the Duke of Northumberland stepped forward.

"Lady Jane, may I present my son, Guildford Dudley."

They're so unalike! thought Jane. Northumberland was dark haired, gruff and robust whereas this preening boy was a dandy. She racked her brains for anything she knew about Northumberland's family... She was sure he had many children, mostly married, so Guildford must be at least his fourth or fifth son. But why would her parents have settled for such a junior member of the family? And hadn't she once heard Mistress Ellen say that he was reckoned to be a useless lad, more interested in clothes than anything else?

"Have you nothing to say?" asked her mother sternly.

"Pleased to meet you, my Lord," Jane mumbled, conscious that her cheeks were hot with embarrassment.

The young man looked at Jane down his nose. He was clearly as unhappy with their betrothal as she was.

"Likewise," he said coldly.

"Very good," Northumberland spoke as if the exchange of these few words meant everything was agreed. "Now we must sort out the arrangements. I suggest the twenty-first of May."

The twenty-first of May! Jane was stunned. *That's less than two weeks away!*

"Father, that will never give my tailor enough time to make my clothes," Dudley whined in a high voice that set Jane's teeth on edge. She was liking him less each second.

"*We* can be ready by then," said Lady Dorset smugly.

"Well from the look of her, Jane does not have quite my standards," sneered Dudley. "And with her height, she's not going to need a lot of cloth."

"Guildford, stop," warned Northumberland. "You'll do as I say. The twenty-first of May it is. And the wedding will be at my home."

"Durham House will be perfect," agreed Lady Dorset. "Why don't I accompany you and Dudley to your rooms and we can discuss the details?"

As soon as they were gone, Jane was on her knees.

"Father, can't it be delayed?" she begged. She was hoping desperately that if her father agreed, there was at least a chance something or somebody would try and stop this wretched marriage ... perhaps even Guildford Dudley himself. "I need time to get used to the idea."

"I'm afraid not," Lord Dorset said firmly.

"But engagements are usually much longer. Father, please think about it."

"I can't."

"Why?"

"Because your wedding must take place before Edward dies."

Jane was bewildered.

"Why?" she asked again.

"The king is determined that a new-religionist should succeed him. Mary is Catholic and Elizabeth is a bastard so he has chosen you instead."

"Me? Queen?"

Jane was aghast. It had never occurred to her that Edward's death would mean she would inherit the crown. She felt dizzy with fear.

"Father, please, no!" she begged.

"I can do nothing. It is the wish of the king."

"The king..." Jane didn't believe that. He had looked far too ill to make such a decision. Then she remembered Northumberland and his whispers in the poor boy's ear.

"Don't you mean it is the wish of Northumberland?" she said accusingly.

Suddenly everything was falling into place. Edward was so weak the duke ruled the country in all but name. But once the king died neither Princess Mary nor Elizabeth would allow this to continue so someone else must inherit the throne if he were to cling to power. And who better than a fifteen-year-old girl, married to his son? But Jane wouldn't accept the throne. She didn't want it and it was wrong. Even though Mary was Catholic, she was King Henry VIII's eldest daughter. The crown belonged to her.

"What does it matter whose wish it is?" snapped her father. "It's your chance."

But Jane knew it was a chance she must refuse even if it meant defying her parents.

"I won't do it," she said forcefully.

"It's too late. Edward's will is being rewritten as we speak. It will be witnessed by the Council tonight."

"Then someone will have to change it," cried Jane. "Even you, mother and Northumberland can't crown me against my will."

"**Will** you agree?"

"No."

Jane felt another blow to the backs of her thighs.

Earlier that evening Lord Dorset had summoned his wife and Jane had never seen her mother so furious.

"Is it true?" she'd demanded, lips tight with rage.

Jane was terrified. She'd never defied her parents before but now she knew she must find the strength. She couldn't be queen.

"Yes, Mother," she had answered, her voice trembling. "I won't marry if it means I'll be crowned."

Lady Dorset's grey eyes had bulged.

"You'll do as we tell you." And she had struck Jane full in the face with a leather glove.

The pain was excruciating. Nauseous, Jane had sunk to the bench but her mother had set upon her in a frenzied rage, pushing her down and grabbing her ankles.

"Tie her up," she had ordered and Jane found herself face down on the floor with her hands and ankles bound to the ends of the bench. Lady Dorset had whipped her bare legs over and over again with a birch rod until they were raw and bloody. But still Jane refused. She wouldn't do it and they couldn't make her. It was a battle of wills.

"You must," said Lady Dorset.

"No."

"For the last time, tell me you will," yelled her mother, wrenching Jane's head around so they were eyeball to eyeball. Jane was exhausted but she wouldn't give in.

"I can't," she groaned.

"Henry, tighten the cords."

Lord Dorset pulled himself from his chair and fumbled with the ropes.

Jane screamed as the cord cut into her wrists.

"Now will you agree?"

"No."

"Arrgh!" shrieked Lady Dorset in frustration. She was panting heavily and patches of sweat discoloured her crimson silk gown. "We're not getting anywhere like this."

"Northumberland will think we're fools if we can't control our own daughter," said her husband wearily.

"Then we'll have to find another way. Let's leave her tied to the bench for the night. By morning, she'll be begging for mercy."

Moments later the key turned in the lock. Someone tried the handle, checking the door was fastened, and Jane was left alone in the cold, dark room.

27

"**Miss**, are you all right?"

Jane was freezing and her muscles were painfully cramped but somehow she'd fallen asleep and now she must be dreaming.

"Miss, it's me."

There it was again... She wasn't dreaming. Someone was calling her ... from the window.

She shuffled round on the wooden floor, dragging the bench with her, till she could see a black hood at the glass casement. And then the window was pulled open and Maud's face appeared.

"Are you alone, miss?" Her maid peered anxiously inside.

"Yes," said Jane and a moment later Maud threw in a bundle and clambered over the window sill.

"Quick. We haven't got long."

"What are you doing?"

"I'm getting you out of here," said Maud, frantically cutting at the cords with a small penknife. "After what I heard last night ... your screams and their cruelty ... your mother and father aren't fit to be parents. There. Can you stand?"

Slowly Jane forced herself up. She was stiff with cold, her wrists and ankles ached, the cords had left deep dents in her skin, and her hands and feet were numb.

"I'll try," she said, shuffling to her knees, feeling giddy. "Hold on."

"I can't, miss," said Maud, hauling Jane to her feet. "There isn't time. Now put this on. You can't go anywhere in that fine dress."

Jane felt too weak to do anything, but she was determined to pull herself together. She picked up the bundle. It was a long black cloak with a hood made from scratchy wool wrapped around a patched grey dress. With Maud's help, she unbuttoned her gown and flannel petticoats and pulled on the shabby clothes. As she did so, her fingers brushed against the cross Katherine had given her and she tucked it under her collar.

"This way, miss." Below the window was a wooden ladder, about ten feet tall, leaning against the palace wall. "Climb down."

"Where are we going?" asked Jane.

A rooster crowed in the early morning light.

"I'll tell you later."

Suddenly Jane felt it didn't matter where Maud was taking her as long as she escaped from her parents, Northumberland and their awful plots and schemes.

Despite her painful legs, she managed to climb out of the narrow window and down onto the towpath that ran the length of the palace.

"Don't make a sound," breathed Maud, pointing at the windows above. "And watch out for soldiers."

Silently they hurried away, staying close to the wall. At any moment Jane expected to see guards or hear shouts, but luck was with them.

"There he is," said Maud, pointing to a narrow jetty. Moored at the end was a fishing boat, and a man in a baggy blue shirt stood poised with an oar in each hand.

"Who is he?" asked Jane.

Her maid was silent.

"Tell me," she insisted.

Maud bit her lip. "Forgive me, miss, it's Ferdinand. I didn't know what else to do so yesterday evening I went and found him at the Carpenters' Guild."

Jane was furious.

"I told you I never wanted to see him again."

"There was no one else."

"But he's Catholic."

"So what?"

"So it will be a trap."

"Of course it won't," said Maud, her temper rising. "He's your friend and he's risking his neck for you."

"If he's Catholic, he's evil," said Jane, a little less certainly.

Maud took a deep breath. "Don't be so ridiculous. Was I evil before Lord Ware told us to change religion? Were my parents? And the old king? There are good and bad Catholics just like there are good and bad new-religionists. And I'm certain Ferdinand is a good person, whatever you think of him."

Jane was startled; Maud had never spoken to her like this before. And there was truth in what she was saying. Ferdinand *had* helped her out of London all those years ago and now here he was again despite her abandoning him in that monastery without saying a word. Suddenly she was ashamed.

"Maud, I've been an idiot," she said simply. "Do you think he'll ever forgive me?"

Her maid smiled. "Now's the time to find out."

And together they ran down the jetty to the little boat and freedom.

28

Ferdinand steered the boat expertly into the centre of the river, where it picked up the westward current.

"It's good to see you again," said Jane as soon as they were safely on their way. "And I'm sorry for the way I left you. I've been so stupid."

"It doesn't matter." Ferdinand's voice took her by surprise. It was deeper than she remembered and gruffer. And that wasn't the only thing. His face was longer and leaner, his eyebrows heavier, and his whole body had filled out. He was a man now, not the boy she remembered.

"Has Maud told you of our plan?" he asked as he tugged at the oars.

Jane shook her head.

"Do you remember that morning when you broke the curfew? You told me that you wanted to disappear rather than go home and stupidly I persuaded you out of it. Is it still what you want?"

"Oh yes!" said Jane, hugging her knees. Just the thought of it made her glow. If she disappeared she would never be sold, crowned or forced to marry Guildford Dudley. She would be free.

"Even though it will be difficult?"

"No matter how hard it is."

"Then that's what we are going to do. There are always maids coming and going. With a bit of luck I should be able to get you a position in one of the kitchens, close to the Carpenters' Guild. We might even find a place where you and Maud can work together."

By the time they moored the boat on a small quay at the bottom of Pudding Lane, it was almost midday. Ahead was a narrow street, with timber and daub houses so closely crowded together that the windows on the overhanging second floors were only feet apart.

Ferdinand knocked on the first door, a busy bakery.

"Do you need any help in the kitchen?" he enquired, pointing at the two girls.

A rotund man with a floury apron shook his head. "No thank you, son."

Ferdinand tried the next door and the next until he reached the last house in the street, where a bent old lady with a pointed nose and sharp cheekbones answered.

"Madam, could you do with any help?" asked Ferdinand. "These two are good workers. They could take some of the load off you."

The woman eyed Maud and Jane suspiciously.

"They don't look up to much."

"Oh but we are," ventured Maud. "I'm very strong – I can carry heavy loads and buckets from the well and I never complain."

Jane knew she ought to say something ... but what useful thing could she do? Then she remembered all those mornings she had spent embroidering with the dowager queen.

"And I can mend and sew," she added.

"How many different stitches do you know?" asked the old lady.

Jane frowned as she tried to remember.

"Cross stitch, blanket stitch, chain stitch, lock stitch, tapestry and cable knitting. That's all, I think," she answered, hoping this would be enough to impress.

The woman rubbed her chin thoughtfully.

"Then you might both be of use to my daughter. Mistress Peasecod is her name. She and her husband are tailors and they live above their shop on London Bridge, two down from the Thomas of Becket Chapel. Tell her Mistress Nonsuch sent you."

Despite her painful legs and arms, Jane hurried eastwards along Thames Street with Maud and Ferdinand until they reached Fish Street.

"This way," said Ferdinand.

Ahead was London Bridge, the only bridge in the city. It had twenty stone arches and grand shops selling silks, wool, silver and gold, and it teemed with peddlers, vagabonds, flocks of sheep and geese, wealthy merchants and scurrying maids.

They pushed their way through the bustling crowd until they reached the church.

"That must be it," said Ferdinand, pointing to a shop crammed with bolts of silk, taffeta, damask and velvet of every colour. Above it was a narrow but elegant four-storey house with a neat front door and a shiny brass knocker.

The girls climbed five steep steps and rapped on the door. A woman answered. She had the same nose and prominent cheekbones as her mother but was more finely dressed with a stiff ruff and fitted girdle.

"What can I do for you?" she asked, holding a handkerchief to her nose.

"Mistress Nonsuch sent us," said Maud. "She thought you might be looking for maids, particularly ones who sew."

The woman looked at them suspiciously.

"I am looking for two girls," she conceded. "How old are you?"

"Fifteen and seventeen," answered Jane.

"And do you have any recommendations?"

"No, ma'am," said Maud. "We've just come from the country, but I promise you, we're hardworking. We can cook, clean, wash, fetch and carry, and Jane is excellent with a needle."

The woman looked thoughtful.

"I'll give you a week's trial. If I'm happy, I'll pay fifteen shillings plus food and lodgings."

Jane saw Maud hesitate. Fifteen shillings was insulting. It should have been twenty. But they needed a roof over their heads. Maud turned to Jane. "What do you think?"

"We'll take it."

"Good," said Mistress Peasecod. "You might as well get started straight away. You'll have every fourth Sunday afternoon off starting with St Bede's."

Ferdinand was waiting for them at the bottom of the steps.

"She'll take us!" said Jane excitedly. "We start today. Thank you so much."

He smiled. "Well done. Now I should get back to the Guild or I'll be in trouble. When is your day off?"

Jane told him.

"I'll collect you then, at two o'clock. Good luck and in the meantime, if you need me, I'm working on a new house near Southwark Cathedral."

29

"*Time* to get up, Jane."

Jane opened her eyes. She was lying next to Maud on a lumpy straw mattress in the corner of an attic. The room was crammed with blankets, linen sheets, silks, tablecloths and boxes filled with lace, buttons and cotton reels of every colour.

Jane rolled onto her stomach and peered through the tiny window. The river swirled below, creating great eddies as it rushed through London Bridge's narrow arches, and the sky was still grey. It must be before five in the morning.

"Why so early?" she moaned.

"Remember, Master Peasecod has an important guest for supper today. Cook says there's a lot to be done or we'll never be ready in time."

Drowsily, Jane stretched. Her body still ached from her mother's awful beating and on top of that for six days she'd worked from dawn until dusk, running backwards and forwards along the busy bridge to the Fish Street well, emptying chamber pots into the river and turning the spit in the baking kitchen for hour upon hour, and then in the evening sewing and mending until her eyes were tired and it was too dark to see. The soft skin on her palms was blistered and she was permanently exhausted yet she couldn't slack. She and Maud were on trial and Mistress Peasecod kept a watchful eye.

Jane climbed out of bed, pulled on her skirt and blouse, slipped on her clogs and walked downstairs yawning.

The kitchen was behind the shop, overhanging the river. It was a stuffy room, its walls hung with forks, knives, skimmers, saucepans and skewers. In one corner was a pile of logs for the oven and in the other a large wooden table.

"Right you two, get working," said the cook, a short, bony man with a bushy black beard and two fingers missing on his right hand. "Jane, that pheasant needs plucking. Maud, cut the fruit and I'll get on with the pies."

"What are we making?" enquired Jane.

"Venison, roast pheasant and swan, custards, jelly, pottage, beef stew and strawberries."

It sounded almost as grand as the banquets at Greenwich Palace.

"Goodness. Who's coming?" she asked.

"I don't know. Someone important from the city. Now stop gossiping and get on with your work."

It took Jane ages to pluck the pheasant and the swan, and then she had to knead dough for bread and chop huge quantities of leeks, onions and cabbage. Although she was hot and tired she reminded herself that, although this life was hard, it was better than the one she'd left behind.

Late in the afternoon, the cook announced, "Jane, Maud, clean yourselves up. The mistress wants to see you."

It's the end of our trial, thought Jane apprehensively. *She's going to give us her decision.*

Quickly, she and Maud dipped a cloth in a bucket of water and washed their faces, necks and hands before hurrying next door to the shop where a customer was paying for two yards of tulle. Once Mistress Peasecod had wrapped the cloth in paper and seen the customer to the door, she came over looking harried.

"So far you have both done well enough but I want you, Jane, to serve a meal before I make up my mind. You'll wait at our table tonight. Do you think you can manage?"

"Yes, ma'am."

"Good. Then put on a clean pinafore and watch your manners. We've fine company so nothing must go wrong."

Less than half an hour later, the kitchen bell rang and Jane picked up a great pie.

"Hurry back for the rest before it gets cold," instructed the cook, holding open the door.

Carefully she climbed the narrow stairs to the dining room. It was a plain room, furnished only with an oak table, two benches and a dresser. The Peasecods were seated on one side of the table, both in their finest silks. Mistress Peasecod was in garish yellow, fidgeting nervously with her uncomfortable but fashionable ruff.

Meanwhile, her husband was laughing overly loudly. He was clearly in awe of their guest. Jane glanced at the man inspiring such admiration. He was elderly with hair as white as the swan she'd plucked for supper and from his waist dangled a sword and a shiny dagger.

A grand soldier, Jane decided as she set down the heavy pie dish.

"What's this?" the man asked.

As he spoke, Jane saw a lump, the size of her fist, on his neck and suddenly a chill ran down her spine. It was Sir John Brydges, the man who'd arrested Sir Thomas Seymour in the middle of the night.

"Jane, you heard the question," said Mistress Peasecod sternly. "Pray tell us what it is."

This was getting worse. Now he knew her name.

"It's quince and beef pie, ma'am," she answered, eyes to the floor.

"Made by you?" asked the man.

She glanced up. Sir John was staring at her intently.

"No, we have a fine cook," interrupted Mistress Peasecod, fluttering a fan. "Jane is a new girl. She's been here just under a week."

Jane's heart sank. Could Sir John have heard of her disappearance from Greenwich Palace? Might he be suspicious?

"Get on with it, girl," said Mistress Peasecod. "Bring the rest of the food. We don't want to keep our guest waiting."

Jane hurried from the room. *You're being ridiculous,* she told herself. *You're invisible to someone like him.* But as she closed the door she heard Sir John enquire, "Did you say that girl was new? Tell me, what's her surname and where is she from?"

She must get away. There was no time to lose.

"**Take** the stew and the jellies," ordered the cook when Jane returned to the kitchen.

"The mistress wants Maud to bring a jug of beer," said Jane.

"Why? I left one on the dresser."

"It's finished. Maud, come on. Mistress Peasecod doesn't like to be kept waiting."

As soon as they were in the hall she turned to Maud. "We have to go – now!"

"Why?"

"Their guest recognized me. It's Sir John Brydges ... the lieutenant from the Tower."

"Jane, where are you?" called Mistress Peasecod tetchily.

"On my way," Jane called back. Then she dumped the casserole and plate of jellies on the floor. "Come on, Maud!"

And together she and Maud slipped out of the front door.

They hurried south along the busy bridge.

"We must get away from London," said Jane. "Too many people know me here. The only thing is Ferdinand.

It's not right to disppear again after everything he's done for me."

"Then let's tell him on the way," said Maud. "He's working close to Southwark Cathedral – it can't be far."

Several times Jane glanced anxiously over her shoulder, but there was no sign of Sir John Brydges or the Peasecods. They crossed the drawbridge and found themselves in Southwark, a bustling village with timber houses, tree-shaded inns and a honey-coloured cathedral.

"Could that be it?" Jane pointed to the timber frame of a half-built house only yards from the great church.

Several apprentices dressed in blue shirts and britches were swarming over the frame with hammers, chisels and axes.

"There he is!" said Maud excitedly.

Ferdinand was sawing an oak beam but hurried over when he saw them.

"Has something happened?" he asked, shaking the sawdust from his curly hair.

Quickly, Jane explained.

"And you weren't followed?"

"I don't think so."

"Then hide in the trees by the jetty." Ferdinand pointed to a distant field where the sails of three windmills turned lazily in the evening breeze. "The master will be along soon and then I'll be finished for the day."

Jane and Maud ran along a muddy towpath towards the meadow. The jetty, which they could see at the far side of the field between several tall elms, was rickety and weather-beaten with a battered rowing boat tied to its end.

They huddled behind the thickest tree trunk.

"We need to find somewhere more remote..." Maud said when she had got her breath back. Then she smiled. "Somewhere like my village! It's way over in the west, in Devon. You'd never be found there. It's the quietest place."

"I couldn't ask your parents to keep me."

"They wouldn't have to. It's not long until harvest, when farmers are always looking for extra hands."

"Are you sure?" asked Jane.

"'Course I am. We can be there within the week."

Just then they saw Ferdinand in the distance, walking towards them.

"Let's go meet him and tell him our plan," said Jane.

They were hurrying back along the towpath when Jane noticed two soldiers coming up behind Ferdinand and catching him up fast. Her heart started thumping. *It's just a coincidence*, she told herself. Then, on the far side of the field, she saw four more soldiers and from behind the middle windmill several more emerged with Sir John Brydges shouting orders. They were trapped and this time there would be no escape.

31

"**We're** surrounded!" said Jane. "Maud, Ferdinand, run! It's me they want, not you."

But it was too late. The soldiers were now less than a hundred yards away.

"Don't move!" shouted Sir John.

Jane grabbed the others and pulled them behind her as she raced towards the jetty.

"The boat!" she shouted. "It's our only chance."

They sprinted across the damp grass.

"After them!" shouted Sir John.

Jane glanced over her shoulder. The men were getting closer every moment.

With his long legs, Ferdinand reached the jetty before them and began loosening the boat's ropes.

"You can make it!" he shouted. "Come on!"

Jane grabbed Maud's hand and tugged her along. The soldiers were only fifty yards behind them and closing the gap fast, but they could still make it.

"Not far to go," panted Jane, when suddenly Maud tripped and tumbled to the ground, taking her mistress with her.

Jane struggled to her feet but it was too late. A soldier

grabbed her ankle and another caught Maud's arm.

Frantically Jane turned to the Ferdinand.

"Go without us," she shouted. "There's nothing you can do!"

She could see the indecision in his eyes.

"Go!" she screamed.

"Fire, you idiots!" called Sir John. "Don't let him get away!"

Ferdinand ducked as an arrow struck the side of the boat and then another streaked past only inches from his shoulder.

He'll never make it, thought Jane desperately.

Another volley of arrows flew through the air and suddenly the boat flipped over and Ferdinand disappeared.

"He's jumped in the water," shouted one of the soldiers.

Ferdinand surfaced, thrashing in the water, but the tide was pulling him further and further from the shore.

"Fire!" shouted Sir John Brydges but he was out of range.

"The bleeder's got away," grumbled one of the soldiers as Ferdinand disappeared round the bend in the river.

"No he hasn't," said Sir John. "The current will take him. He doesn't stand a chance."

He looked down at Jane.

"Get to your feet, miss. There are a couple of people I know who will be very relieved to have you back."

"*If* Jane disappears again, I will hold you personally responsible, Mistress Ellen," declared Lady Dorset as she marched out of the room, bolting the door behind her.

The nurse picked up a dress of raw gold silk. "Let's get you ready, miss."

Without a word, Jane put it on and then sat silently in front of the glass while Mistress Ellen braided pearls into her hair.

"On my life you've never looked lovelier, miss."

Jane knew her old nurse was trying to cheer her up but it didn't help. She'd never been so unhappy.

At three o'clock her parents returned. Lord Dorset wore a knee-length green satin jacket buttoned with jewels. Her mother was even more splendid in red and silver with an underskirt that shimmered as she moved. Both were flushed with excitement. As soon as Edward died, the crown would fall into their laps.

"Let's go," said Lord Dorset. "We mustn't keep everyone waiting."

Moments later, Jane found herself at the entrance to a magnificent hall crammed with people.

"Remember Maud," hissed her mother as three

trumpeters saluted their arrival.

The evening Sir John Brydges had delivered Jane back to Greenwich Palace, Lady Dorset had given her an ultimatum. Marry Guildford Dudley and accept the crown and Maud would go free. Refuse – and Maud would die. Jane had no choice.

A last shrill trumpet note echoed around the hall and the gossiping courtiers separated right and left, creating an aisle from the doorway to a small platform where Northumberland, his son and a priest were waiting.

The duke was dressed soberly in a suit of black silk but Dudley could not have been gaudier. His doublet was sewn from the same cloth as Jane's dress, his hose was white and very short and gold tassels dangled from his ankles, elbows and cuffs.

Miserably, Jane followed her parents. In only a few minutes she would make her marriage vows to this showy boy and then there would be no going back.

"No kiss from my loving bride?" whispered Dudley sarcastically as she stepped onto the dais. "Am I really so awful you had to run away?"

Jane kept her face blank.

"Not even a peck on the cheek?" he asked, puckering his lips.

Jane's tears welled up.

"Enough." Northumberland growled. "Let's get on with it, Archbishop."

"Will you both kneel?" said the priest.

Jane sank down onto a red velvet cushion, shuffling as far away from Dudley as she could.

"We are gathered here in the sight of God," rumbled the priest, "to join this man and this woman in holy matrimony. If anybody here knows of any reason why these two may not lawfully be joined in marriage, speak now or forever hold your peace."

Just for a moment Jane hoped someone would stand up and say that it was wrong, that she was being forced into this marriage against her will. But there was nothing but a terrible silence.

"Guildford Dudley, wilt thou have this women to be thy wedded wife? Wilt thou love her, comfort her, honour and keep her in sickness and in health so long as you both shall live?" said the priest.

"I will."

Jane felt a tear roll down her cheek. It was almost done.

"And Lady Jane Grey, will you take this man to be thy wedded husband? Wilt thou obey him, serve him, love, honour and keep him in sickness and in health so long as you both shall live?"

Jane looked up but she couldn't speak.

"Remember your maid," whispered Lady Dorset.

She forced out the words. "I will."

"Those whom God hath joined together, let no man put asunder. I pronounce you man and wife."

It was done. She was married and there was no escape.

33

"*Get* up, Jane!" shrieked Lady Dorset. "Northumberland is on his way."

Jane pulled the blankets up to her chin. He had finally come to fetch her. But she wouldn't go. She had promised to marry Guildford Dudley but she hadn't promised to live with him. Once the wedding was over and all the guests had departed she'd refused to stay at Durham House a moment longer. She'd cried so piteously that at last Northumberland had made a grudging proposal. "I'll give her time but I want her close to London. Syon House will do." That had been six weeks ago and the duke must have decided her time was up.

"Get up, if you ever want to see Maud again. And come to the parlour in half an hour or there'll be trouble."

Reluctantly Jane did as she was told. But when she knocked on the parlour door, it was not her mother who answered.

"Come in," said a gruff voice.

Cautiously she opened the door and was astonished to find a room crowded with courtiers, all of whom were bowing in her direction.

"What is this?" she asked.

Northumberland stepped forward. He looked grave and was dressed from head to toe in black.

"King Edward died three days ago, your Majesty. You are now our sovereign and our queen."

Ever since her marriage, Jane had dreaded this moment. Morning and evening she had fervently prayed for the king's recovery but her prayers had been in vain.

"It cannot be true," she begged.

"I have the proof with me." Northumberland held up a parchment scroll tied with a red ribbon. "This is Edward's last will, signed in his own hand. Now do your duty."

Jane sank weakly to the ground. "I can't," she said, as the room began to spin.

"Wake up, Jane!"

Someone was shaking her shoulder. She had no idea where she was or what was going on.

"Come on, you stupid girl."

And then she smelt burning and opened her eyes. Her head was resting on a table and someone – her mother – was holding lighted feathers under her nose.

"What happened?" she asked.

"You fainted."

And then Jane remembered. It wasn't a nightmare, it was real – she was queen. Her head felt as heavy as a cannonball but she managed to sit up. She was still in the parlour but now she was alone except for her mother and the duke.

"She is all right now," said Lady Dorset.

"Well she's going to have to do better than that next time," Lord Northumberland grumbled. "We leave for London tomorrow and we can't have her falling over every time someone reminds her she's queen. Believe me, there are others who are not so squeamish about occupying the throne."

"Princess Mary?" snapped Lady Dorset. "Surely your men have captured her by now."

"It's not that easy," answered the duke. "Somehow she got news of Edward's death and fled to Norfolk before I could do anything about it."

"And Elizabeth? Tell me you've got her locked up."

"She's at Hatfield. She's too ill to travel."

"Too ill, my foot," retorted Lady Dorset. "This is becoming a shambles."

"That's why Jane must play her part."

"I'll manage Jane. But you must take better care of everything else."

Manage me... Manage me... That's all my mother ever does, thought Jane bitterly. She had to stop it.

"I can't go to London," she said simply.

Lady Dorset was startled.

"You'll do as I tell you."

"I won't." Didn't they understand? She couldn't be queen. The prospect terrified her, but more than that, it was wrong. "Mother, please listen to me."

But her mother, furious, slapped her cheek hard.

"Lady Dorset, control yourself!" said Northumberland. "Remember, Jane's the queen."

"How else can I make her behave?"

The duke looked worried.

"Is there anybody she's close to?" he asked. "Someone we could make her lady-in-waiting... Keep her in good spirits until we've captured Mary and Elizabeth?"

"There's nobody suitable," said Lady Dorset. "The only person she cares about is her maid."

"And where is her maid?" asked Northumberland impatiently.

"Locked in the cellar, your Grace."

"Maud's here?" gasped Jane. She couldn't believe it. For the past six weeks she'd longed to see her.

"She is reviving already," said the duke. "Fetch this maid at once."

Jane waited for what felt like hours until at last Maud was hauled into the room. She flung her arms round her maid. "Maud! Are you all right?"

"I am well, miss," said Maud, but she didn't look well. She looked pale, frightened and terribly thin.

"What have you done to her?" Jane asked her mother.

"Nothing. She needs food, that's all."

"You haven't fed her?"

"Of course I have," answered Lady Dorset. "But I can't afford to dole out too much to girls who aren't working."

"Now you are queen, you can stop this happening," smiled Northumberland.

"I will never be queen," said Jane.

The duke shook his head disbelievingly.

"Don't you realize it's too late? Your reign has begun. It is your duty to take the throne or there'll be trouble." He stared at her grimly. "Terrible trouble. For you, as well as for me and for this Maud you're so fond of."

Jane could see he meant every word. She was trapped and Northumberland knew it.

"Lady Dorset," he said, "see that they are both ready first thing in the morning and get the maid something decent to wear. We leave for London at dawn."

34

"*I'm* sending you away," said Jane as soon as she and Maud were alone.

"No, miss," said Maud firmly. "I won't leave you again."

"It's too dangerous. If Northumberland's plot fails, I'll be killed. Princess Mary will have no choice. And she will turn on my servants as well."

"I will take the risk," said Maud. "Honestly. It's what I want."

"Thank you," said Jane. "You are the only person I can trust. But you stay on one condition. If I ever tell you to go again, you will leave straight away."

"Miss, I told you I want to stay."

"I know. But you must promise me," said Jane. After what had happened to Ferdinand, she was determined not to risk another friend's life.

Her mistress looked so resolute and sad that Maud relented. "If it makes you happy, then I promise," she said quietly.

The next morning they were up before dawn. Jane wore a green and gold velvet gown and a matching hood and, for the first time, Maud was almost as grand. A lady-in-waiting couldn't wear a brown wool dress, apron, cap and clogs, so Jane had given her three other gowns: one of blue velvet, another of burgundy damask and the one Maud had picked for today, a grey silk dress with black trimming around the bodice.

"What do you think?" asked Jane, pulling Maud in front of the glass.

Maud stroked the soft folds of the robe.

"I can't believe it's me," she said. "Even my mother wouldn't know me. I look like a lady."

"You are a lady," said Jane. "My lady-in-waiting, Mistress Maud Scythe! Now we must go."

They hurried through the Syon House gardens. Waiting by the river were Lord and Lady Dorset, Northumberland, several courtiers and Dudley. Jane hadn't seen her husband since their wedding but he was still a preening fool fussily instructing a servant where to stack his luggage. *Is this really the man I'm to spend the rest of my life with?* she thought sadly.

"You're late," said her mother. "This is an important day, so don't mess it up."

As she spoke a green and gilt barge came round the bend in the river. It had two decks and a luxurious cabin with glass windows, and was rowed by twenty oarsmen dressed in scarlet.

"The royal barge, your Majesty," said Northumberland, making a great show of his bow. "Guildford, you two will share the cabin."

Jane couldn't bear the thought of sitting next to Dudley, not when she would have to pass under London Bridge, right by the very spot where Ferdinand had slipped into the river. And surely a queen could choose her own company.

"I'm sure Lord Dudley would enjoy the journey more outside with the other men, Northumberland," she said in a clear voice. "My lady-in-waiting will amuse me instead."

The duke scowled, his thick eyebrows twitching in irritation, but he could not overrule an order issued in public by his new sovereign.

"As you wish, your Majesty. But by the time we reach London, your husband should be at your side. It is what your people will expect."

Jane knew she had pushed him far enough.

"Guildford may join me once the Tower is in sight," she said as she stepped aboard.

At least then she would be past London Bridge.

They glided downriver, between fields of ripening corn and orchards of apples, pears and cherries. There were few boats out so early in the morning, only the occasional fisherman throwing a line, but as they got closer to London the river was busier, with cargo boats loaded with coal, wheat and stone, fancy wherries and tiny ferries rowing one or two passengers from one side to the other. Hamlets turned into villages and then into grand villas and gardens until at last Jane saw the towers of Westminster Abbey and beyond them the city walls.

If only I hadn't gone to him for help, Jane thought for the umpteenth time as they passed the field with the three windmills and the ricketty jetty.

"I'm certain Ferdinand survived, miss," said Maud, reading her mistress's mind. "I can feel it."

"I wish I could be as sure," said Jane sadly.

Just then Northumberland and Dudley appeared at the entrance to the cabin.

"Your Majesty, the Tower is in sight."

Jane sighed. "Maud, please wait outside."

Dudley threw himself down on a cushion and put his arm around her shoulders. His touch made her skin crawl.

"How soon will we be crowned?" he asked.

"What do you mean 'we'?" said Jane irritably, inching away from him.

Dudley smiled.

"You don't think my father's risked everything just to make you queen? A girl can't rule alone. You need a man at your side – your husband."

Jane was furious. It was bad enough that she had been forced to marry this appalling, vain boor but she would never allow him to be king.

"Don't be ridiculous. A king inherits the throne. You have no claim to it."

"You have the royal blood and I have the power."

"I won't allow it," said Jane.

"We'll see about that, won't we?" said Dudley

provocatively. "Now don't look so glum; we're nearly there."

The walls of the Tower of London loomed ahead of them. Its quay was decorated with coloured flags that fluttered in the afternoon breeze but it was still a sombre place and the tiny crowd did nothing to lift Jane's spirits.

"Make way for Queen Jane," boomed a chamberlain as she stepped ashore under a gold canopy.

But as she walked with Dudley towards a large gate no one cheered and no one waved, not even the children. It was a dismal reception. *These people know I'm not their true sovereign*, thought Jane as the Tower gate clanked ominously shut behind her. *How is Northumberland ever going to make this work?*

It was a muggy summer's evening.

"Your Majesty, Lady Dorset is here to see you," announced a red-faced guard.

"Show her in."

Jane put down the book she'd been reading to distract herself. She had now been staying in the White Keep for over a week. On the day they arrived at the Tower there had been a furious row. Dudley had run straight to his father, snivelling that Jane wouldn't allow him to be crowned and of course Northumberland had been livid. What sort of ungrateful wife was she, to deny her husband? But Jane had been adamant and in the end Northumberland had stormed out and she'd hardly seen him or her parents since.

"The duke has left."

Lady Dorset looked dreadful. Her eyes were puffy, her skin grey and she was sweating heavily in the stifling heat.

Jane was startled. "Why?"

"He's gone to fight Princess Mary. She's raised an army in Norfolk."

"Will he win?" Jane half dreaded the answer.

Her mother pulled out a handkerchief and patted her

forehead. "No... Everything's gone wrong. I should have known you'd never be strong enough to pull this off."

Jane was stung by the unfairness.

"It's not my fault," she protested. "I never wanted to be queen."

Her mother shrugged indifferently.

"A different person might have succeeded. Now all I can do is beg Mary's forgiveness and pray."

"What about me?"

Lady Dorset reached for the door handle.

"You are on your own."

Jane paced the room, her mind racing. Mary could already be victorious and, if so, how long would it be before she came here, to claim the Tower? She pushed open a shutter, half expecting to see the new queen galloping across the drawbridge, but the castle's grassy courtyard, thick walls and moat were still and quiet in the fading light.

Maud came in. "It's so sticky, we need a storm," she said, not daring to mention what was on both of their minds. Then she frowned, seeing Jane's plate of congealing mutton. "Your Majesty, you haven't eaten any supper."

"I'm not hungry."

"But you must keep up your strength. I'll go and find you some fruit. That'll be easier to swallow."

Despite its rich hangings and carpets, the royal apartment was gloomy and oppressive, and Jane was relieved when Maud returned. But as soon as she saw her ashen face, she knew something was wrong.

"What is it?" she asked.

"Your Majesty, there's nobody here. I've looked everywhere – the kitchens, the flesh larder, the garderobe, even the cellar."

"What do you mean?"

"I can't find a soul. Even your rooms are unguarded. What's happening?"

Instinctively Jane knew. Her allies deserting her could only mean one thing.

"I'm not 'your Majesty' any more," she said quietly. "Northumberland's been defeated. It's all over for me."

36

"**Save** yourself, miss. Tell Mary this plot was nothing to do with you. She knows what Northumberland and your parents are like."

But Jane shook her head. "It's hopeless. She can't forgive me – I took her throne."

"No you didn't. Your parents and the duke did."

"In my name."

"And you were forced to go along with it," said Maud. "Please, miss. We can still get away! Everyone else has managed to escape and we can too."

Just then a distant bell began to toll, followed by another and another. Jane ran to the window. All over the city bonfires were being lit and now it seemed the bells in every church were ringing.

"Is London under attack?" asked Maud nervously.

"London is celebrating," said Jane. "Mary is coming."

"Then there's not a moment to lose." Maud grabbed Jane's hand and together they ran down a steep spiral staircase.

They were several turns down when they heard the sound of hooves clattering on stone. Jane stopped at a small casement in the stairwell. The courtyard below was filling with hundreds of soldiers on horseback. Many more were pouring across the drawbridge.

Sir John Brydges's gravelly tones echoed around the stone turret. "I swear she's in here, your Highness. My guards would never have let her get away."

"Your Highness"! Mary is only feet away! thought Jane.

Together, she and Maud ran back upstairs, two steps at a time.

"Through the hall," Jane panted at the first landing. "If we go any higher we'll be trapped in the White Keep."

They veered off into a large deserted chamber whose painted walls were lit by flickering torches. On the far side was a single door.

"This way," said Jane, and they found themselves in a dark passageway.

"I don't like it," muttered Maud and then she shrieked as a high-pitched voice called out, "Who's there?"

Jane peered into the gloom. Ahead of them was a tiny girl, not more than six years' old, with straw-coloured hair, wide eyes and a pinched face.

"Who are you?" she asked.

"My name is Bess Colt."

The girl was shaking.

"What are you doing here?"

"Waiting for my mother. She's gone to fetch our things and then we're leaving, just like everybody else, but I'm scared." The girl's eyes welled with tears. "This corridor is haunted."

"No it isn't," said Jane, trying to reassure the frightened child.

"It is." The girl wiped her nose on her sleeve. "By Queen Anne Boleyn. Ever since she died her ghost has stalked this place ... pacing from her bedroom as far as that hall with a candle in her hand ... only she's got nothing from the neck up."

Maud gulped.

"I reckon she's already taken my mother," continued the weeping girl. "She said she'd only be a few minutes but she's been gone for ages."

"There must be another way out." Maud was as white as a sheet.

Jane pulled her close and whispered, "It won't be a ghost that's got her mother. It will be Mary's men. We can't leave her here." She turned back to the child. "Bess, did your mother tell you the way out?"

"Yes. She said beyond the old queen's rooms is Salt Tower and at the bottom is Iron Gate. She said it was guarded, but the guards have run off."

"Then that's where we'll take you," said Jane.

"I can't leave," protested the child. "My mother told me to wait."

"Your mother may be a little while yet," Jane said as gently as she could. "But we'll look after you. Isn't that better than waiting here, all by yourself?"

Reluctantly, the frightened little girl nodded.

Jane, Maud and Bess hurried down the dismal passageway.

"Queen Anne's bedchamber is on the other side of this door," whispered Bess. "But her room's haunted worst of all."

"It will be fine," said Jane, but she couldn't help feeling uneasy. The air was so humid and heavy, and this part of the Tower felt so abandoned.

Just then there was an almighty bang and Maud and Bess screamed.

"It's just thunder," said Jane. "Now the storm has started at least it will cool down." But her hands were shaking as she lifted the catch. Bess's talk of headless ghosts had unsettled her.

The room ahead was alarmingly dark.

"I can't see a thing," whimpered Bess, clutching Jane's arm.

There was another boom of thunder and several lightning flashes, one after another. The eerie flickering revealed an enormous chamber with a tiled floor, a high ceiling decorated with tiny coats of arms, and three large windows. It must have been fit for a queen once, but now it was dusty and stale, and there wasn't a stick of furniture in it.

"Nobody's used this room since she was beheaded," whispered Bess as rain began thudding down outside. "The king forbade it."

Jane shuddered, picturing the doomed Queen Anne Boleyn pacing the room.

Another booming explosion was followed by several more flashes of light. Quickly Jane scanned the panelled walls. There were two doors, on either side of a marble fireplace and, if Bess was right, one of them must lead to Salt Tower and freedom.

She opened the door to the left of the fireplace but it was impossible to see where it led.

"Wait here," she said, shuffling forward and cursing herself for not having grabbed a torch in the Great Hall when she had the chance.

Her foot struck against something hard. She bent down and felt stone steps – but they were going up. Surely the way out must be down.

She headed back to the chamber.

"It must be the other door," she said.

Neither Bess nor Maud responded. Perhaps they hadn't heard her over the cascade of rain. But then she saw they were staring across the room, transfixed. On the far side of the chamber was the unmistakeable silhouette of a woman.

38

"*It's* Queen Anne," sobbed Maud. "We should never have come this way."

Jane felt dizzy. In the darkness she thought she saw the figure crouching down. And then there was a spark.

"She's lighting a candle," whispered Bess. "That's what the headless ghost always carries."

But another flash of lightning showed them that the woman on the far side of the room wasn't headless at all. Instead she had a long hood and was richly dressed in a full-skirted scarlet gown, and she was bending down, struggling with a tinderbox. There was another flash, and Jane could see her pale skin and coal-black eyes. She was in her early twenties ... much too young to be Mary. Suddenly Jane knew who it was... Elizabeth. The princess must have arrived with Mary's men and taken the opportunity to visit her mother's rooms. At any moment she would light that torch. Jane had to do something before Elizabeth saw her.

She pulled the others towards the untried door, praying the pelting rain would cover any noise.

"Who's there?" The princess sounded alarmed.

As Jane lifted the catch on the door there was another

spark and a tiny glow; the wick of Elizabeth's candle was alight.

"Go," Jane whispered, pushing Maud and Bess through the doorway.

"And you," protested Maud.

"No."

"I'm not abandoning you."

"Maud, remember your promise," said Jane.

"Who is it?" Elizabeth called out imperiously, and now the light from the candle was getting stronger and closer.

Jane pulled Katherine's cross from her neck and thrust it into Maud's hand.

"Use this... Sell it to help you. For my sake, go." And she shut the door.

"Speak to me," ordered the princess, holding up the light.

Jane walked forwards.

"You!" said Elizabeth. "I should have known! Trying to escape, were you? Well, I swore I'd get my revenge and here's my chance."

As her fingers closesd on Jane's arm, several soldiers rushed into the room. Behind them was Sir John Brydges.

"Your Highness," said the lieutenant with relief. "I've had men searching for you everywhere."

"Well, it appears they are not doing a very good job," said Elizabeth curtly. "Look who I've found. She almost escaped."

She pushed Jane forward.

Sir John looked appalled.

"I don't know how this could have happened, your Highness. I thought Lady Jane was in her apartments in the White Tower."

"You'd better lock her up or Queen Mary will never forgive you."

"Yes, your Highness."

Sir John gestured to his men.

"Lady Jane Grey, you are under arrest."

But Jane didn't care. Ferdinand had paid a terrible price but Maud was free.

The Tower of London, 12th February 1554

"**Come** away from the window," begged Mistress Ellen.

"No," said Jane. "I have to know what to expect."

She was dressed in a long plain robe, a hood and a cape of black crepe. Northumberland had been executed and today Queen Mary had ordered Jane's death, straight after the beheading of Guildford Dudley.

The clock tower struck and Dudley came out of Beauchamp Tower, directly opposite the cramped rooms where Jane had been kept with her old nurse since her arrest. He was dressed in plain black clothes, so different from his usual gaudy suits, and was clutching a Bible to his chest.

As he emerged into the bright morning light he glanced up at her window. Jane withdrew slightly. She didn't want to be caught spying on him. All she wanted was to prepare herself for what lay ahead; she mustn't beg for mercy, or cry. She must die with dignity. It was all she had left.

Her husband looked pale, with dark bruises under his eyes. His shoulders slumped as two soldiers grabbed his arms and marched him away. *I'll never see him again*, thought Jane. It was so strange and unreal, she hardly knew what to feel.

Some time later, she didn't know how long, she heard the roar of a distant crowd. Guildford Dudley must be dead and now it was her turn.

"Are you ready?" asked Mistress Ellen.

Her nurse was also dressed in mourning clothes. She looked tired and worn – a spent old lady.

"Yes," said Jane softly.

"Then we should go."

Jane found she could hardly put one foot in front of the other. *Be calm*, she told herself. *There's not long to go.*

At the bottom of the spiral staircase was a small door. Sir John Brydges was waiting for them outside in a narrow cobbled road between the battlements. His eyes were cold and hard as he inspected the two women.

"Follow me," he said, turning towards an arch opposite Traitor's Gate. "And Lady Jane, today you will do exactly as I tell you."

They were halfway along the road when a wooden cart came trundling towards them.

Mistress Ellen pulled Jane against the wall as it squeezed past. "Miss, don't look!"

But it was too late; Jane had already seen Dudley's lifeless body lying on top of a thin layer of straw. Blood was oozing from his grotesquely severed neck and beside it was a lump wrapped in dirty linen that was stained red.

"Surely you could have taken the body out the other way," protested Mistress Ellen. "Have pity on the poor child."

Jane closed her eyes and breathed slowly and deeply, trying to calm her nerves, but it didn't help. She couldn't do this.

"Come on, Lady Jane," said Sir John brusquely.

Mistress Ellen dabbed her eyes. "Hold my hand, miss."

They continuted down the winding street and through the gate onto Tower Green. The large courtyard was much more crowded than Jane had expected. Hundreds of people were pushing and shoving for the best view. Among them were were soldiers, butchers, merchants, beggars and young girls with baskets of dried lavender. Mothers holding babies and fathers carrying curious pointing children on their shoulders. Even the high battlements were lined several rows deep.

"No point waiting," said Sir John. "There'll be riots if this lot don't get to see what they've come for."

Jane passed through the gate and the chattering crowd fell silent. It made her feel lonelier still. No one here cared for her. All they wanted was the hideous thrill of witnessing an execution – and not a normal execution. The execution of a queen.

A soldier began to bang a slow, steady beat on a large copper drum. The sound echoed around the courtyard and Jane found herself walking in step with it towards a wooden scaffold on the far side of the green. It was six feet above the ground, and leant against the west wall of the White Tower.

Once again she felt horribly light-headed. The scaffold was less than a hundred yards away. These were the last steps of her life.

"This way, miss." A soldier pointed at some rough wooden stairs.

Jane climbed onto the platform. There, in the middle, was a large wooden block and behind it stood her executioner. The man was dressed in a black tunic, a leather apron and a macabre mask that covered his face from his forehead to his top lip with slits for his eyes. But worst of all, in his shovel-like hands was an axe, its polished blade gleaming in the watery sun.

Tears pricked Jane's eyes. *Don't cry*, she told herself. *Be brave.*

She took a moment to steady herself, then turned towards the sea of sombre faces. The drummer fell silent.

"Lady Jane Grey has been found guilty of treason," announced Sir John Brydges in a booming voice. "Her Majesty, Mary, Queen of England and Wales, has decreed that she should be executed for her crimes." He turned to Jane. "Before you die, madam, is there anything you would like to say?"

Jane knew she must beg God's forgiveness but her mouth was dry. She swallowed but found it impossible to speak.

"Lady Jane?" said the lieutenant gruffly.

In her panic she stared at the hushed crowd and then a movement caught her eye. Two figures, high on a battlement, were signalling to her. One of them was small and wore a white cap. The other was tall and dark. The small one was Maud and, beside her ... could it really be ... Ferdinand! And Jane was no longer alone.

"Lady Jane, you've had your time," said Sir John sternly.

"No," she said quickly, finding her voice. "Please, let me at least say my prayers."

She fell to her knees.

"God, have mercy upon me," she implored in a loud clear voice. "Although my crime was great, no one can ever say that I sought the crown or was pleased with it. And now good people, help me with your prayers."

"Madam, are you ready?" asked Sir John curtly.

Jane nodded.

With trembling hands, she pulled off her headdress and handed it to her nurse.

"Mistress Ellen, come away," said Sir John from the back of the platform.

The nurse shuffled towards him with tears streaming down her cheeks, leaving Jane alone with her executioner.

From behind the mask came a gruff request. "I beg your forgiveness for what I have been commanded to do."

"I give it willingly," said Jane automatically, and was

surprised to find that she meant the age-old words.

The executioner lowered his voice, so that only she could hear.

"Kneel on the straw in front of the block, and for God's sake, keep still. I'll do my best to make it quick."

Jane felt giddy. This was really it. She was about to die. Tears pricked her eyes. *No!* she thought and she looked up at Maud and Ferdinand. Then she raised a hand to tell them she was grateful they'd come.

"None of that, madam," growled Sir John from the far side of the platform. "Where's the handkerchief?"

"Here, sir." Mistress Ellen pulled a strip of linen from her pocket.

"I don't want it," said Jane, desperate to see her friends for as long as possible.

"It's the rules," said Sir John firmly and he handed the cloth to the executioner.

The handkerchief was tied tightly around Jane's temple. Now she couldn't see a thing.

"Dispatch me quickly," she called out to the executioner, and she reached for the block. But, blinded and confused, she couldn't find it. Suddenly she was terrified he would strike before she was ready. Before she could be sure to be still.

"What shall I do?" she called out. "Where is it?"

"Let me help her," she heard Mistress Ellen plead. There were footsteps and Jane felt her head being gently guided onto the block and her plait pulled to one side, exposing her neck to the chill winter air.

This is it, she thought. *Lord, into thy hands I commend my spirit.*

And the axe came down.

The End

What Happened Next

Lady Jane Grey was executed at the Tower of London on the morning of 12 February 1554. She was just sixteen years' old and had ruled as queen for only nine days.

She was not immediately buried. Instead, her butchered body was left lying on the scaffold. That evening her head was thrown into a pit with that of Guildford Dudley, and the rest of her corpse was lowered into a grave beneath the Church of St Peter ad Vincula on Tower Green, where it joined the bones of two other headless queens – Henry VIII's second and fifth wives, Anne Boleyn and Catherine Howard.

Jane's father, Lord Dorset, was beheaded one week later. His wife was luckier. Lady Dorset made no attempt to plead with Queen Mary for either her daughter's or her husband's lives. Instead, three weeks after Lord Dorset's death, she shocked the English court by marrying a young servant called Adrian Stokes. She probably arranged this demeaning marriage to ensure she was no longer a threat to the throne. If this was her strategy, it paid off, for shortly afterwards she was pardoned by Queen Mary and allowed to return to court. Here she took the precaution of never mentioning Jane again, as indifferent to her daughter in death as she had been in life.

In her old age she grew increasingly fat. She died on 20 November 1559, and was buried in Westminster Abbey.

Queen Mary was now the undisputed monarch but her reign was not a happy one. She was determined to crush the new Protestant faith and return England to Catholicism. Against the wishes of many of her people, she persuaded Parliament to repeal all Protestant laws. Opponents of Catholicism were condemned as heretics. Many were burned at the stake, dying in agony, earning the queen the nickname "Bloody Mary".

Mary made her unpopularity worse by marrying Philip II of Spain. Her subjects had no wish to see either a Catholic or a foreigner on the throne. Despite these objections, the wedding went ahead on 25 July 1554, in Winchester Cathedral.

The marriage was doomed from the start. The couple were badly matched. Philip was a handsome young man of twenty-seven whereas the queen was twelve years older and in ill health. Mary soon convinced herself she was pregnant, but this proved a false hope. After a second phantom pregnancy, Philip returned to Spain leaving Mary heartbroken.

The queen's health had never been good and now she began to suffer terrible stomach pains – probably caused by cancer. These got worse and by 1558, Mary knew she was dying. Arrangements needed to be made for her succession. Desperately she tried to convert Princess Elizabeth to the Catholic faith. Despite her sister's refusal, on 6 November 1558, Mary recognized Elizabeth as her heir. The queen died eleven days later. She was forty-two and had reigned for only five years.

Elizabeth ascended the throne at the age of twenty-five. She was to reign for the next forty-five years, a golden age that became known as the Elizabethan Era. This period is famous for its drama, above all for the plays of William Shakespeare, the seafaring exploits of adventurers such as Sir Francis Drake, and the defeat of the Spanish Armada in 1588, one of the great victories in English history. However, Queen Elizabeth's finest achievement was to largely settle the religious question that had caused such strife during the reigns of her father, brother and sister, and the nine-day reign of her cousin, Lady Jane Grey.

Queen Elizabeth was the last of the Tudor monarchs. She never married, perhaps chastened by the disgust at her affair with Sir Thomas Seymour. Instead she declared, "I have already joined myself in marriage to a husband, namely the Kingdom of England." She died on 24 March 1603 at Richmond Palace and is buried in Westminster Abbey.

At the end of her long reign Elizabeth was succeeded by James I, the King of Scotland. He was the son of Mary, Queen of Scots and the great-grandson of Margaret Tudor. Margaret Tudor was the sister that King Henry

VIII disinherited in his will over fifty years earlier – the decision that caused young Lady Jane Grey to be so fatally elevated in the succession for the throne of England and Wales.

Author's Notes

When I first began to research the life of Lady Jane Grey, I was delighted by how many historical resources there were to draw on. Her family were Tudor aristocracy and, as Edward VI became frailer, Lady Jane Grey's importance grew and therefore much was written about her and the many key members of the Tudor court with whom she overlapped, including Katherine Parr, Sir Thomas Seymour, Princess Mary, Princess Elizabeth, the Duke of Northumberland, Guildford Dudley, the Dorsets and King Edward. In addition many of her letters have survived and some of the houses she lived in can still be visited today.

There is, however, one glaring gap. No authenticated portrait of her exists. Instead I have relied on a description given by a Genoese merchant who was present in the crowd when she was brought to the Tower of London shortly after the death of Edward VI. He wrote, "This Jane is very short and thin ... she has small features and a well-made nose, the mouth flexible and the lips red. Her eyes are sparkling and hazel in colour." He added that her complexion was freckled and her teeth were white and sharp.

When writing this story I have tried to make sure that I have been accurate about the history of the period and the key characters in Lady Jane Grey's short life.

One area where I have simplified things is in my use of titles. Tudor nobles often changed their names. For example, Somerset started life as plain Edward Seymour and was made to Earl of Thetford when King Henry VIII married his sister Jane Seymour, finally becoming the Duke of Somerset when he ruled for Edward VI, the boy-king. Similarly his brother, Thomas Seymour, became the Lord Admiral at the time of Jane Seymour's royal marriage and Lord Sudeley when his nephew inherited the throne. Northumberland was born John Dudley. An excellent soldier, he became Viscount Lisle under King Henry, Earl of Warwick at the beginning of Edward's reign and then Duke of Northumberland once he had brought down his arch rival, the Duke of Somerset. Jane's father was born Henry Grey. He became the Marquis of Dorset when his father died and later Duke of Suffolk when he conspired with Northumberland to put Jane on the throne. To avoid unnecessary confusion, throughout this book I have used the name by which the person is most commonly remembered.

I have also had to imagine the characters of some of the main players. We do have some clues from the past. Lady Dorset was a cruel mother who beat Jane at the slightest excuse. When Jane was thirteen, she complained to her tutor that she was "sharply taunted" by her mother and that she "pinches, nips and bobs ... that I think of myself in hell." Lord Dorset was wealthy but not especially talented. Despite his marriage to King Henry VIII's niece he was not awarded any significant position at the Tudor court and was described by an imperial ambassador as being "an [protestant] ideologue without sense." Thomas Seymour was "one of the prettiest men at court" but, as Princess Elizabeth remarked on hearing of his execution, "this day died a man with much wit and very little judgement." Elizabeth was prickly as a result of being described for most of her childhood as a "little bastard" and "the daughter of a whore". Queen Katherine Parr was a gentle woman who did much to unite the unhappy children of Henry VIII. And Jane so loathed Guildford Dudley she refused to have him crowned.

Of Jane's character we have much evidence. She is described as being solemn and clever. She was an able scholar in Latin, Greek and Hebrew as well as studying Arabic, Italian and French. She was also a committed new-religionist with a strong sense of right and wrong, and certainly had no desire to inherit the crown. Witnesses record that when she was told of her deadly inheritance she fell to the ground overcome with shock and distress. But whatever her personal characteristics, what determined her fate above all else was her royal blood. Once King Edward fell seriously ill, the ambitions of the Duke of Northumberland and her unscrupulous parents ensured she was doomed. When their plot failed, the only thing left to her was to die with dignity. The records of eyewitnesses present at her execution are heartbreaking to read but provide evidence that this, at least, she achieved.

Notes from the Past

Childbirth: During the Tudor age pregnancy was a perilous affair and it was common for women to die in childbirth, even queens like Katherine Parr and Jane Seymour. This was as a result of poor hygiene leading to infection.

To prepare a wealthy woman for childbirth, the windows of her bedchamber were covered with black cloth to keep out "dangerous vapours". In this dark quiet room the mother would wait for labour. Once the baby was born, she wouldn't leave her chamber for up to a month. At the end of this lying-in, a service of thanksgiving was held and the new mother was blessed with holy water.

Childhood: Tudor parents raised their children with little display of affection, believing this would spoil them. It was commonly held that girls should be treated particularly harshly for, while leniency was bad for sons, "it utterly destroyeth daughters". Lady Dorset's cruelty to Jane was therefore in keeping with the age; however, she was particularly strict and unpleasant.

Sale of children: The Dorsets' sale of their ten-year-old daughter for £2,000 to Sir Thomas Seymour would not have been regarded as unusual in an age when marriage was primarily a business arrangement. Once a child was sold, any income earned from the child belonged to the purchaser. The purchaser usually arranged a marriage and received any marriage settlement from the husband's family. Sir Thomas Seymour believed he had a good chance of marrying Lady Jane Grey to King Edward. If he had succeeded, he might have made a handsome profit.

Apprentices and the Guilds: The London guilds controlled all trade in the city. There were guilds for bakers, drapers, masons, clock-workers, ironmongers, goldsmiths, tailors, vintners, mercers and butchers. Every year each guild would admit around fifty boys. These apprentices took an oath to their masters – to serve him, keep his secrets, obey his commands and not to play cards, go to taverns or get drunk – and in return the master would feed and clothe the apprentice, provide him with lodgings and teach him his chosen trade.

At the end of seven years, the apprenticeship was complete and the apprentice would be a "freeman". He could then wear the silk hood and fur-lined robes of his guild, buy property and, most important of all, start a business of his own.

The Carpenters' Guild: The earliest written record of this guild is in 1271, when the guild was established to look after the welfare, training and interests of carpenters – one of many ancient guilds set up at this time. It received its coat of arms in 1466. This is made up of a carpenter's tools and an upside-down "v", which probably represents a roof rafter.

The Great Fire in 1666 started in Pudding Lane and destroyed most of London's timber buildings. In the wake of this catastrophe, London's citizens decided to rebuild the city in brick and stone. This reduced demand for woodworkers and the Carpenters' Guild began to decline in importance. However it still exists today, supporting the carpentry trade through training and charitable donations.

The Curfew: Tudor London was surrounded by thick medieval walls with seven gates – Aldgate, Ludgate, Bishopsgate, Moorgate, Cripplegate, Aldersgate and Newgate – names still used in the city today. Gates were used to display the bodies of criminals, particularly those accused of treason. They were closed every night when the church bells rang the curfew at dusk, and opened again at sunrise the next morning.

During the curfew nobody was allowed out on the streets of the city. This was to avoid trouble and reduce crime. Nightwatchmen enforced this law and severely punished anyone caught out after dark.

The plague: During the Middle Ages, plague often swept across Europe. Symptoms included swellings in the neck, groin and armpits, and death was usually swift and painful. The worst effects were felt in cities, where people lived crowded together in filthy conditions. In 1563 historians estimate that one quarter of London's population died from a bout of the plague.

Tudor doctors had no understanding of how the plague was caught, blaming it on unhealthy vapours. Victims of the disease had to stay at home, their front doors chalked with the words, "Lord, have mercy upon us". However the wealthy would often flee to their country estates.

Executions: The punishment for treason was to be hung, drawn and quartered, a hideously painful death. The victim was cut from the hanging noose when still alive and then his stomach was split by a knife and he was cut into pieces. Exceptions were made for royalty and nobles. Queen Anne Boleyn opted to be beheaded by a swordsman from France. Lady Jane Grey was killed by the axe, a mercifully swift death as long as the executioner struck firmly.

The English Reformation: In the middle of the sixteenth century, King Henry VIII forced the country to change from the Catholic religion to Protestantism in order that he could divorce his first wife, Catherine of Aragon, and marry his second, Anne Boleyn. This period is known as the English Reformation and it made huge changes to people's lives. Over 850 monasteries were closed. The monarch became head of the new Church of England, rather than the Pope. Most importantly, the style of worship changed.

Protestants objected to many of the ancient practices of the Catholic church such as the selling of indulgences and pardons (rich people would donate money to the church and in return their sins would be forgiven), the venerating of relics and shrines, and the belief in trans-substantiation (Catholics believe that during the Communion service, the bread and wine blessed by the priest become the actual body and blood of Christ whereas Protestants believe the bread and wine is symbolic).

Protestant changes meant that churches and services became plainer. Statues were destroyed, wall paintings whitewashed and stained glass windows smashed.

Protestants: In Tudor times, Protestants such as Lady Jane Grey were called "new-religionists". This term was later switched to "Protestants" as the new-religionists were protesting against some of the practices of the Catholic Church.

Religious language: Up until the middle of the sixteenth century, priests held church services in Latin, a language few spoke, and people could be burned at the stake for possessing an English Bible.

A key idea of the Reformation was that religion should be understandable and so, for the first time, Bibles written in English were placed in churches throughout the land.

Catholic resistance: The changes brought about by the English Reformation were not popular with everyone. During the reigns of Henry VIII and Edward VI, Catholics who refused to convert to the new religion were called recusants and were severely punished. Despite this, some Catholic priests continued to practise the old rites. However they had to do so in secret, moving from the households of one sympathiser to the next or meeting in out-of-the-way places.

Rosary beads: During the Tudor period, before the English Reformation, rosary beads became a popular aid to prayer and remain so to this day in the Catholic faith. A rosary is made up of five groups of ten beads, known as a decade, often with a cross hanging at the end.

During Tudor times, wealthy people had rosary beads made of gold and precious jewels. Poorer Catholics would have made do with wood. After the Reformation, rosary beads were frowned on by the new-religionists.

Before they were famous ... meet Cleopatra, who will one day be the Queen of Egypt.

As a young girl she flees Alexandria, fearing for her life. Living in hiding, uncertain of her future, she finally receives news from home. The time has come to face her enemies – and take her place as Princess Cleopatra, future Queen of Egypt.

"Gives a flavour of the times while delivering a first-rate story."
Publishing News

BY CAROLINE CORBY

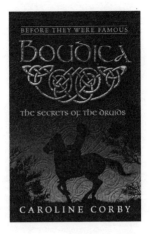

Before they were famous ... Meet Boudica, one day to be England's warrior queen.

As a tribesman's daughter in Ancient Britain, Boudica is in trouble. The Romans have invaded, her father has been accused of murder and she doesn't know who to trust. When a mysterious druid appears in her village, she knows she must enter his murky world if she is to bring honour to her tribe.

BY CAROLINE CORBY

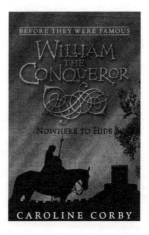

Before they were famous ... Meet Willam, one day to be William the Conqueror, Duke of Normandy.

Medieval France is shocked when the son of a peasant is chosen as Duke of Normandy. Powerful families plan to murder the boy and steal his title. He runs for his life, but when there's nowhere else to hide, it's time to face his enemies and become William the Conqueror.

<u>BY CAROLINE CORBY</u>

Before they were famous ... Meet Pocahontas, who saved the first English colony in Virginia and shaped the destiny of her people for ever.

The Native Americans of Virginia had a prophecy – that one day strangers would come to Chesapeake Bay and destroy them. So when a group of English settlers land, Chief Powhatan forbids his people to approach them. But his daughter Pocahontas is too curious to obey. Are the mysterious pale men to be trusted or will the terrifying prophecy come true?

BY CAROLINE CORBY